MW01051669

THE WHISK OF *Love*

ELAINE HOOVER

Order this book online at www.trafford.com
or email orders@trafford.com

Most Trafford titles are also available at major online book retailers.

© Copyright 2011 Elaine E. Hoover.
All rights reserved. No part of this publication may be reproduced, stored in a retrieval
system, or transmitted, in any form or by any means, electronic, mechanical, photocopying,
recording, or otherwise, without the written prior permission of the author.

Author Credits: front cover sketch by Hannah Jane Withers, Artist

This is a work of fiction. Names, characters, places and incidents either are the
product of the author's imagination or are used fictitiously. Any resemblance to
actual persons, living or dead, events, or locales, is entirely coincidental.

Printed in the United States of America.

ISBN: 978-1-4269-7070-2 (sc)
ISBN: 978-1-4269-7071-9 (hc)
ISBN: 978-1-4269-7072-6 (e)

Library of Congress Control Number: 2011913322

Trafford rev. 07/23/2011

 www.trafford.com

North America & international
toll-free: 1 888 232 4444 (USA & Canada)
phone: 250 383 6864 ♦ fax: 812 355 4082

FOR MONICA "MUNKA", OUR RAINBOW GUARDIAN
ANGEL

FOR HANNAH JANE, MY PRIDE AND JOY

I paid mom money
I paid mom bread
I paid mom everything
For what she said
    Elaine Hoover, Second Grade

I'm going down to the river bank this morning
Way before the family is awake
Gonna lay me down at the foot of the water
And spill out all my troubles for everyone's sake

You can't have love when you never can surrender
I've been spreading around my anger like a plague
I've sailed this far with my boat on fire
Fighting flames each day, too stubborn to expire

I will soak my soul
Let the river take control
Let the river take control
I know it's not too late
To let go the weight
To let go the weight

The sun will rise and shine on me this morning
It will seep its way into my heart
And untie all the knots that have hardened me through the years
And I'll embrace wisdom that sun will impart

And with this heat burning inside me
I will warm all of the people that I love
In their darkest of hours and weakest of minds
I'll light up their nights with every star I can find

I will soak my soul
Let the river take control
Let the river take control
I know it's not too late
To let go the weight
To let go the weight
    Ari Hest,
    The Weight

DECEMBER 30–TUESDAY
DAYS TILL MUSIC CRUISE = 75
BRAD'S THOUGHTS=OFF HER RADAR
MARCIA'S BEVVIE-OF-THE-MOMENT=STRONG FRENCH ROAST WITH 1/2 & 1/2
BRANDI'S LYRICS (VIA HEADPHONES) THAT GET HER THRU=YOU CAN'T BREAK A HEART THAT WASN'T EVEN YOURS TO BREAK

The tastefully wrapped Xmas gift that had, on a whim, accompanied her on the Saturday morning blind coffee date at the Bridge Street Deli now sat complacently on her kitchen counter. The gift box contained a scalp massager, which could be used to decompress after a long, stressful work day. It looked a lot like a normal kitchen whisk, except that the bottom was open-ended. When a person used the scalp whisk on someone else's head, the results were amazing. It was a life-saver. The whisk even had romantic potential, as in get your date nice and relaxed…But Marcia had decided against presenting it to her date at their initial meeting. It was too much, too soon (the story of her life).

The way things had been going since that enjoyable first "meet for coffee" date; Brad was NEVER going to get that Xmas prize. Brad was NEVER going to get that Xmas prize because he had already gotten homemade Norwegian butter cookies (norsk smorkranz) AND a cup of whipped-cream-free hot chocolate. And after careful scrutiny (READ: review the DISASTER DATE file), Marcia decided that those two items were sufficient first date booty. After all, what, exactly, had SHE gotten (other than heartache and pain?). And by now (almost 1.5 weeks later), it was obvious to even her that she and Brad were never meant to share cold Wisconsin winter nights together, whisking each other's scalps.

In fact, her dreams of one day becoming a top-producing-scalp-whisk-sales rep had now been dashed. How could she possibly spend her days on Wisconsin back roads, delivering record-setting quantities of scalp whisks to unsuspecting WI residences, when thoughts of "what-might-have-been-with-Brad" would cause her to go skidding out of control on the black ice in her small Civic Hybrid, projectile-launching into a 4-foot snow bank, causing her to sustain additional bruising to her already-black-and-blue heart? He was certainly NOT worth losing her life or even her mental health over.

Marcia was, at present, navigating a WI back road. County Road H, to be precise. At least, she thought it was County Road H. The optometrist had botched her eyeglass prescription, so the sign, when she passed it, was somewhat blurry.

RANDOM THOUGHT: Marcia took pride in the fact that the state of Wisconsin constructed all of their road sign posts with wood, not metal. And they were not draining their entire supply of hazel nut trees doing it, either.

Marcia had, earlier that day, picked up a fresh supply of scalp whisks from the "Whisks R Us" warehouse in Minneapolis. She was now en route from Minneapolis to Haystack, making a few deliveries along the way. It was an ambitious schedule for a Tuesday.

She was drained from having driven the 44-mile stretch of MN Highway 65. Travel was, by far, the biggest "con" of her whisk rep job. Every time she drove that dang Highway 65, Marcia literally took her life into her own hands. It was bad enough that there was congestion equal to CA Highway 1 on the road. It was also December in the Midwest and the temps had FINALLY fallen below zero. That meant two things:

1. As a small Hybrid driver, she had to be extra careful to avoid the dozens of snowmobilers that were attempting to cross the highway. It was a harrowing "game" of maneuvering the Hybrid between the Ski Doo's (that traveled horizontally) and the black ice (that covered the road vertically). Fortunately for Marcia, the riders all wore fluorescent SKI DOO gear and helmets for visibility. She had already mentally noted that Neon Green was a popular color for SKI DOO apparel that year.
2. Equally challenging was the task of avoiding the monster Ford F150 trucks on the road. Most of these trucks had ice houses hastily loaded onto their attached flatbed trailers. Small Hybrid cars (READ: Marcia, in particular, with her European scarf/urban appeal/flashy earring) did not have a chance in hell against said trucks. Forget "Minnesota-nice" when it came to these particular

Fords (and their drivers). The moment they saw that "H" (Honda) on Marcia's spoiler, the trouble began.

Strangely, it did not seem to matter one iota that her Civic Hybrid had been built somewhere in Alabama, U.S.A. The offending Ford F150 extended cab would go from being one mile behind Marcia to "in her face" aka "on her trunk" in a matter of 44 seconds. Also, it did not matter if she, like the Ford truck, was currently passing cars in the left lane at 85 MPH. The big bad TRUCK would be sure to "gun it" to 90 MPH, even 100 MPH. Simply for the thrill of trying to force the innocent Hybrid off the road.

Marcia made a mental note to check into the purchase of an added battery pack for the Hybrid. Perhaps this would help to rectify the Ford truck situation?

The Hwy 65 icehouses, themselves...heck, it did not matter if they were not SECURELY attached. Remember, one of the 10,000 MN lakes was calling the icehouse owner's name and EVERYBODY ELSE BETTER GET THE HECK OUTTA THEIR WAY! There was only FOUR FRIGGIN' months left to ice fish! There was NO TIME for lollygaggers like Marsha on Highway 65 North. Who gave a rip about saving the planet (dumb Hybrid driver)? Who gave a rip about getting an estimated 3–6 miles to the gallon? Heck, gas, at $3.79 a gallon, was a freaking STEAL. The fishing equipment, the Coors Lite, it was ALL PACKED IN THE TRUCK BED AND ONLY THIRTY-SIX HOURS REMAINED OF THE WEEKEND. There was no time to waste.

The saddest part of it all was that Marcia LOVED to ice fish (well, admittedly, she had only gone ice fishing ONCE in her life but still, she had fond memories of that peaceful outdoor experience). It was just that the whole MN/WI winter experience seemed somehow tainted by this tiny population of beer-laden, beat up, rusted-out or BRAND SPANKING NEW Ford trucks.

DECEMBER 30–TUESDAY (CONTINUED)
DAYS TILL MUSIC CRUISE = 75
MARCIA'S BEVVIE-OF-THE-MOMENT=JOSEPH HOOVER FAMILY MEMENTO BEER MUG FILLED WITH CARIBBEAN RUM (STRAIGHT UP)
BRANDI'S LYRICS (VIA HEADPHONES) THAT GET HER THRU=IN A CROWDED ROOM, I'M ALONE

Marcia was jolted out of her commuter daydreaming the moment her Hybrid reached the bridge spanning the Rum River near Haystack. She always took time to read the familiar sign posted on the bridge. Today Marcia actually did a double-take when she saw the sign, which read "NO JUMPING FROM BRIDGE". Marcia had to question the logic of this sign...it was, after all, the Rum River. Today was the kind of day that MARCIA NEEDED TO BE COMPLETELY IMMERSED IN THE FREAKING RUM RIVER! But only, Marcia reasoned, if it was 100% RUM flowing under the bridge, a GOOD RUM, such as the dark rum her Nassau pal brought back with him to his WI college reunions. Or, better yet, the smooth Caribbean rum that was used in the umbrella-topped Cherry Limeade's that Marcia would soon be drinking on her upcoming music cruise. Marcia decided that if completely immersing herself in the Rum River was not feasible, she could at least console herself that night with the dusty bottle of duty-free Caribbean rum she had stashed in her cupboard.

Marcia smiled at the thought of a strong rum cocktail and hastily completed her last whisk delivery of the day (delivered via mailbox–she could always get away with abusing the U.S. Postal Service on Haystack back roads). A few minutes later, she pulled into the driveway of her modest "DOLL HOUSE" condo. The condo was completely dark for two reasons:

Marcia was "kid-free" for the next six months! Her Daughter, Ana, had recently boarded a plane to Germany on a student foreign exchange program. Marcia was still acclimating to her new status as a single, available woman. Marcia could now have popcorn dinner every freaking night! Grocery shopping had been quickly replaced with a weekly trek to the Haystack Municipal Liquor Store! Marcia promised herself daily to make the most of each free day, now that it was unfettered with kid scheduling.

Marcia also vowed to use this "kid-free" time to purge any lingering DISASTER DATE files from her heart. It was obvious to Marcia that this was the biggest reason her date with Brad had not resulted in a second date. Her head and heart had never found closure from years of heartbreak. If Marcia was able to rid herself of all DISASTER DATE memories, she could free up her emotional state enough to find a B-F-T-W (BOY-FOR-THE-WINTER) while Daughter was away. Marcia and her friend Betty were having a B-F-T-W powwow the very next day to develop local dating prospects. As an added bonus of purging bad dates, Marcia would be completely freed up to "fall hopelessly in love" on her upcoming music cruise. Who knew what kind of amazing man lay in wait for her on the ship! She might even transcend BOY-FOR-THE-WINTER and find BOY-FOR-ALL-SEASONS! She would create a new acronym: B-F-A-S! Marcia never gave up hope. Besides, it was always easier to schedule "male sleepovers" without a kid to complicate matters. Marcia was nothing if not resourceful while her child was away.

Home maintenance was NOT one of Marcia's strong points. The third of three outside lights on her condo had burnt out just the previous night. The chances of Marcia getting out the four-foot step ladder to replace bulbs that night–in minus 22 temps–was very slim. Marcia shivered at the thought.

Besides, Marcia was still traumatized by her last outdoor stepladder experience. The only reason Marcia had been on that dang stepladder at all was that she had (a mere four months after the fact) noticed a hornet's nest the size of Tupelo under the front door eave. So she had perched on the unsteady stepladder, using a rake to simply "rake away" (frantically attack) the hornet's nest. OK, admittedly, it was not the smartest way to attack the healthy nest. But it had saved Marcia a trip to Menard's. Menard's was NOT a store Marcia enjoyed hanging out at. When hornets, both dead & alive, had flown out of the nest, Marcia had gotten startled and lost her balance. The rake (circa. 1948) weighed in at sixteen pounds.

It was only her yoga-balance-poses (which she was quite proficient at) that saved Marcia from serious injury. She caught herself just in time and suffered only a bruised hand (which was easier to contend with than a bruised heart).

Marcia made a mental note to move "DOLL HOUSE condo maintenance" up on her priority list. She sighed at the thought of her TO-DO list and opened her car door. The events of the long day had left a sour taste in her mouth. She was exhausted. If she could just look on the bright side. Her scalp whisk sales were spectacular! Why should she throw away all her "top producer" potential because of a dumb coffee date? The scalp whisks, at $6 a pop, had been one of few hot items during the recession holiday season! Marcia must somehow find the strength to carry on.

One of the first feelings Marcia had when she walked through the door of her condo that night was panic. This was based on her inability to mentally place the Liz Claiborne black-with-white-polka-dot PJ's Santa (aka Marcia) had bought for her to wear while writing her blockbuster novel aka screenplay. The PJ's included a bonus matching sleep mask. Marcia was pretty sure THAT would be gathering dust. But nonetheless… where in the hell were her PJ's? Her Daughter, aka artist-tornado-bedroom, no doubt had something to do with the MIA PJ's.

Marcia definitely needed to de-stress and attempted to open her vial of lavender oil. The vial–Dr. Harvey's Moor Lavender Body Oil–had cost Marcia an astronomical $26.99. Her favorite retail outlet had, of course, been out of Marcia's usual cheaper brand. The well-used bottle of lavender oil, however, was now completely sealed shut. The seal on it was as tight as the seal on the bottle of real, made-in-WI maple syrup that Marcia had sitting in her cupboard.

There was plenty of irony in the fact that the lavender essential oil was supposed to be calming and relaxing and exactly what Marcia needed most at this point in the freaking day.
By now, Marcia was ready to slam the vial of lavender oil against the side of her tub. And then drain the entire $26.99 bottle INTO the tub. And then take a long, hot, bath in the lavender-infused water. Instead, she gently set down the precious vial and decided to get busy.

Once Marcia had located her MIA polka dot PJ's (a mere 1.75 hours later), she retired to her condo crawl-space to find her photo of Munka. Munka was her white-blonde haired guardian angel. The photograph she was looking for showed Munka sitting on the beach, topless, playing in the sand, when she was three years old. The Munka photo, however, was also missing-in-action. MARCIA COULD NOT, FOR THE LIFE OF HER, LOCATE THE DANG MUNKA PHOTO! She desperately needed the photo propped next to her laptop in order to write her blockbuster novel aka screenplay. ARRGGGHHHH. Marcia calmed herself with the thought that there was NO NEED TO STRESS OVER THE MIA PHOTO. MUNKA WAS RIGHT THERE WITH HER IN SPIRIT.

Instead, Marcia found a baseball glove that a former beau had lent to Marcia for her daughter's week at camp. She also came across a ring box from "Attwood England" that she had no memory of purchasing anything from while traveling abroad. Also, third grade mug-shot photos of her daughter and a pal, which were photo-shopped with "DOUBLE TROUBLE" across the top (cuuuuute…). And a battered hard copy of "Eight Cousins" by Louisa May Alcott, which was too old to contain a publication date (in Racine, WI) but had, at one point in time, belonged to a woman named Ann Vander.

Marcia became even more depressed and overwhelmed after digging through the numerous boxes of mementos in her crawl space. Especially when she thought about the "To-Do" list aka the "Marcia-To-Do-List" (M-T-D-L). The M-T-D-L was endless. It would seem that Marcia would make progress on the list, working twenty hours per day. Currently, NO progress was being made. As quickly as Marcia crossed items off the top of the M-T-D-L, new items were added.

For example, Marcia currently had so much clean (washed with Meyer's basil laundry soap, another comfort splurge) folded, laundry stacked on her dryer that she was unable to use the dryer controls to turn the dryer ON. Marcia was constantly changing the dryer setting from high to medium in order to dry her favorite fleece-lined hoodie—or her daughter's endless supply of rainbow-striped legwarmers and tights. She would then forget to change the dryer setting back to HIGH. So a load of laundry could end up taking HOURS at Marcia's house.

She resolved to hire live-in help as soon as she was awarded top whisk sales rep for the year (she was already well on her way and it was only December).

At this point, Marcia decided she would just turn in for the night and try to get up early to work diligently on her blockbuster novel. Now that she was finally in her warm polka dot PJs, Marcia needed to perform her bedtime facial ritual. This involved applying six different types of Dead Sea Salt products: SEA SALT SOAP; SALTY MUD MASK; MINERAL LIFE SERUM; MOISTURING DAY CREAM; INTENSIVE ANTI-WRINKLE CREAM AND MOISTURING NIGHT CREAM.

Marcia looked at the array of beauty products and thought to herself - SCREW IT! She pushed the bottles aside, and got a knife, which she used to tap against the cover of her lavender oil. Miraculously, the vial then opened! Marcia slathered a heavy coating of the lavender oil on her face (how's THAT for a simple beauty routine, she thought) and breathed deeply, trying to wind down.

She realized, with mixed emotions, that it was OK that her coffee date had not worked out. It was all good. Marcia had no room on her memory-foam mattress for a new suitor anyway. Her bed was filled instead with the debris of a creative endeavor, her lifetime dream. Strewn across the bed were draft novel pages, mini zip drives, pens, highlighters, chap sticks, reference novels, pillows and her apple-green laptop, which she had named "Granny" (after Granny Smith Apples and Ana's "GGG", Great-Grandma Garnet). A man, Marcia realized, especially a 6'2" man like Brad, would never fit in her messy bed.

No DISASTER DATE file was closed that night.

JANUARY 2–FRIDAY
DAYS TILL MUSIC CRUISE = 72
MARCIA'S BEVVIE-OF-THE-MOMENT=ICY COSMPOLITANS
WITH A TWIST OF ORANGE PEEL (#1-3)
BRANDI'S LYRICS (VIA HEADPHONES) THAT GET HER
THRU=I'M HAPPY CAN'T YOU SEE, I'M ALRIGHT

Marcia and her pal Betty met at J & J's the next day to map out their
BOY-FOR-THE-WINTER (B-F-T-W) plan. Betty generally had better
B-F-T-W strategies than Marcia. She had an innate way of reading men
that Marcia had to constantly hone. Betty had also invited their monk
friends, Rufus and Anton, to provide male perspective. The monks knew
Betty and Marcia's taste in men well. The term "B-F-T-W" was, after all,
coined for them by Rufus thirty years earlier at a wild college party. The
four friends had been in the same social circle ever since.

J & J's was a one-of-a-kind restaurant located literally in the middle of
nowhere. It provided the perfect atmosphere for B-F-T-W planning. J
& J's menu offered items found nowhere else in WI, such as "Steam
boat rounds served with burgundy mushrooms". J & J's was the kind
of friendly place that offered customers free emery boards (advertising
"Centra-Whisk Coop") from a basket on the hostess stand. Marcia and
Betty could efficiently file their nails while waiting for an available table.
The restaurant also had unique perks like blue "drink chips". Customers
could purchase a "drink chip" when they wanted to buy someone (friend
or stranger) a drink in a non-threatening manner. "Drink chips" could be
used immediately by the recipient or they could be "cashed in" at a future
visit. Marcia and Betty liked J & J's because they received "drink chips"
from elderly farmers on a regular basis.

Today, Rufus, Anton, Marcia and Betty had chosen a dark corner booth
at J & J's so as to be inconspicuous. After all, a prospective B-F-T-W could
walk through the door at any time. Therefore, they all knew it was best
to keep a low profile while maintaining the best vantage point. Scouting
B-F-T-W's was a full-time project.

Alcohol helped to spark their imagination. The table top was littered with
an assortment of half-filled glasses-Bloody Mary's (Betty), heavy-handed-
on-the-rum rum and cokes (Rufus and Anton), and Cosmopolitans

(Marcia). Rufus was currently providing free, unsolicited B-F-T-W advice for Marcia. He had even prepared a list of local "potential" B-F-T-W's for Marcia, which he presented to her on a soggy napkin. Marcia cringed after seeing the list but she remained determined to stay warm that winter, no matter what. It was the only winter she had been "free" in the past fifteen years. She had to start thinking more like Betty. Marcia had never thought in "B-F-T-W" terms before. If she could just forget the old-fashioned notion of a lasting relationship, she could talk herself into doing the B-F-T-W thing. After enough cocktails, a man that had absolutely no appeal on "the list" might magically be transformed into a potential "scalp whisk" partner she could cuzzle with on her couch. Marcia had to ignore her gut feeling that said there was no way in hell she could make the leap from couch to BED with anyone on "the list". Perhaps this was something she could work herself up to–a "B-F-T-W TRIAL" of sorts. Just the fact that she was even listening to Rufus, through a cosmos-induced haze, indicated that she was open to new ideas. Marcia was going to throw caution to the wind for once in her life.

Betty and Rufus were adamantly pitching napkin prospect #1–Irish Bun– as the best potential B-F-T-W for Marcia. He was an "up-north" man whom Rufus knew through the monastery. Irish Bun was big into hunting, fishing and the outdoors. He coincidentally needed a date for the annual Wild Game Feed and Gun Raffle, coming up at J & J's in a few weeks. The timing was perfect. Rufus was extremely confident that Marcia could fill the wild game bill.

Feeling decadent, the four friends indulged in quarter-chicken dinners, surf and turf, Ham and Cheese Balls (with a side of J & J's famous mushroom sauce) and cheesecake. Another round of cocktails was ordered to celebrate the fact that Marcia and her pals would leave J & J's with a definite B-F-T-W PLAN. Irish Bun had unanimously been nominated as the top B-F-T-W candidate for Marcia. They all agreed she had to start somewhere. It was slim pickings in Haystack territory–the B-F-T-W pool was not that deep. Marcia bravely tossed back the last of her Cosmos and fumbled for her coat. Fortunately, Anton was sober enough to serve as the designated driver back to Haystack. After three martinis, Marcia was in no shape to drive–she would be content just to sit in the back seat and attempt to process what she had just gotten herself into.

JANUARY 2–FRIDAY (CONTINUED)
DAYS TILL MUSIC CRUISE = 72
MARCIA'S BEVVIE-OF-THE-MOMENT=ICY COSMPOLITANS WITH A TWIST OF ORANGE PEEL (#4-5) REF: BARTENDER GUIDE 2008
BRANDI'S LYRICS (VIA HEADPHONES) THAT GET HER THRU=IN A CROWDED ROOM, I'M ALONE

Later that evening, Marcia peered out her kitchen window at the Blue Moon. A long stream of light shone mysteriously from one side of the moon. Marcia knew that light represented Munka, her guardian angel, cheering her on. Marcia could NOT slide into a depression–instead, she must try to enjoy a relaxing night home alone. After all, she did not have to cook dinner! Chin up, Bucky, she told herself and she raised her fourth, homemade Cosmo in a silent toast.

If Marcia could sum up how she was feeling right now, she would use the "one earring" analogy. She had driven up Highway 65 the previous day wearing a large gold hoop in only ONE of her ears. (Marcia had lost her other earring when she passed out in front of the cozy fireplace at her little sister's house on New Year's Eve. A mere 40 minutes before 2011 began without her. Marcia couldn't even make it till midnight on New Year's Eve, for cripes sake). Marcia was now feeling exactly as she had felt yesterday on Highway 65–like a loser, a misfit. She felt like she did not fit in ANYWHERE. She knew she had been the ONLY woman driving 65N wearing one earring. It was a perfect reflection of her life. And she was SO self-conscious about it. She had, in fact, adjusted her Hybrid sun visor so that her solo earring would not be quite as visible.

RANDOM THOUGHT: Sun visor use was imperative because western exposure caused sun spots and wrinkles to form on the left side of Marcia's face. Marcia was nothing if not wrinkle-conscious.

Marcia decided she could act as the "POSTER GAL" for all of the "one-earring-ed, single, lonely women" in the entire state of Wisconsin. And Minnesota. But not Iowa. A female pirate kind of look. The "POSTER GAL" poster she would create could even include a photo of Marcia wearing only her one huge (real) gold earring.

As the Pirate-Poster-Gal, Marcia would hide her hair beneath a brightly patterned scarf, with a knot on one side. Because Marcia needed a root touch-up, the scarf would serve more than one purpose. It would be a welcome addition to her wardrobe, as long as the colors "worked".

Marcia made a mental note to start, in her spare freaking time, a new upper-Midwest Lonely Hearts Club called "Pirates of Passion". She would dedicate it to all lonely, single, "feel-like-one-earring-ed in a multiple earring world" people. Heck, even some of the Green Bay Packers wore two lunker "rocks" in their ears! It was just not right.

Marcia sighed and poured herself a fifth Cosmo. She had no time for self-pity. It was time, instead, to review one of her DISASTER DATE files—the STD FILE.

"My," Marcia thought, "What I could do with those initials" but she wasn't going there now.

That night marked nine long years since Marcia had received the Christmas card from STD. She now steadied herself and carefully pulled the card from its envelope. The painstakingly detailed calligraphy on the envelope read: "Happy Holidays—Marcia and Daughter" (one never disclosed their children's names).

Surprisingly, the card itself was not bad—a red and green glittered etching of a gingerbread house. Bonus points for the cupcake, gumdrop and lollipop detail. However, sadly enough, the photo inside the card still had the same shock value as it had had in the year 2001. The photo was disturbing, to say the least—a color Polaroid with four mini, posed head shots. One of these shots had STD covering his face with his hands in a "peek-a-boo" manner—EEEEEEWWWWW. Similar to a photo someone may have taken in one of those curtained photo booths at the MN State Fair. Four mug shots for a buck (and there was usually more than one person in the photos).

The most frightening detail that the photo conveyed were STD's meaty, be-ringed fingers (actually, the rings were not SO bad; in fact, she could potentially incorporate the onyx, garnet and real? gold into her wardrobe somehow). But geeeeez...the guy had to be twenty years her senior, with a prominent double chin to boot. And, wait, no, were those DENTURES? For real?

Based on his head shots, Marcia could only imagine what STD's lower body looked like, in terms of legs and buns and shoes. And couldn't he have selected something more original than a white V-neck T-shirt for his photo shoot? Substandard shirts (READ: not to HER taste) were always a huge red flag for a potential date.

Marcia sighed and slid the card back into its envelope. Had she now stooped to the level of making out with a denture-clad electrician from Droopy Eye, WI? The chances of sparks flying here (no pun intended) were slim. Especially since she now knew she was NOT ever gonna meet STD face-to-face. Not in her lifetime. It was an easy decision for Marcia to make.

In the back of her mind, Marcia had a vague memory of hearing from STD about "the car I'm gonna buy so I can pick you up for a date". Also, a flimsy story about how he and Marcia would not be able to splurge and go to the Bonanza steak house on their first date, after all– his roommate had cleared out the $500 cash he had been systematically stashing in his fridge vegetable crisper for months. "ARE YOU KIDDING ME?" Marcia thought, and she promptly closed the STD file lurking in her head and turned off her bedside lamp.

JANUARY 5–MONDAY
DAYS TILL MUSIC CRUISE = 69
**MARCIA'S BEVVIE-OF-THE-MOMENT = BAILEY'S ON THE
ROCKS THE SIZE OF EAST TEXAS**
BRANDI'S LYRICS (VIA HEADPHONES) THAT GET HER
THRU=IN A CROWDED ROOM, I'M ALONE

Marcia sat alone in her living room the next evening, feeling as blue as the
moon. Even her usual force of angels (Munka and other kind ancestral
spirits) felt weak that night. Marcia glanced up, hoping that the sight of
all her treasured family mementos would help to cheer her up. She saw
instead her only other living room companion, a full-size blow-up male
doll named Milt. Marcia had impulsively purchased "Milt" online from the
"POLYURETHANE PLEASURE" website a few weeks earlier. Marcia
had hoped Milt would act as a male "substitute" of sorts for Sunday
morning cuzzling. Marcia really missed Sunday morning cuzzling with a
man. She had actually tucked Milt into her bed on Saturday night for a
"trial run". Unfortunately, she had awoken the following morning to feel
Milt's cold, rubbery "flesh" pressed against her thigh and screamed in terror.
Milt had felt like a corpse lying next to her. Milt was the farthest thing
from a soothing, warm-blooded male that Marcia had ever experienced.
Since that disastrous night, Milt had been relegated to gather dust in the
living room. He now sat, slumped over, deflated from lack of air, in the
broken-down Barc-A-Lounger. Marcia had decided to bequeath Milt to
Betty, who had expressed interest, despite Milt's lack of warmth and the
fact that Milt was not anatomically correct. The sight of Milt now only
made Marcia feel more depressed.

Marcia realized she needed to place an SOS call (cry) for help to her trusted
pal, Betty. She needed to place that call right now, to take her mind off
Milt.

Comfort–Marcia sought comfort. Betty was not, however, able to provide
much comfort over the phone. Betty deserved bonus points for listening,
for attempting to keep up with Marcia's babbling. However, at the very
moment Marcia called, Betty was sobbing hysterically while watching
"The Bucket List". Betty was lamenting the fact that she, unlike Marcia,
did not have a freaking bucket list. Not even a draft, or at least nothing
in writing.

Betty could never keep up with Marcia because Marcia was a one-of-a-kind-stir-self-into-frenzy piece of work. Betty could, however, relate to Marcia because Betty, herself, had periods of frenzied productivity. Both women had been born under the sign of Cancer in the best year ever–1960. Betty always referred to their insane phases as "manic phases", when sh-- always got done. And right now, Marcia had the bonus force of the Blue Moon. Marcia was getting sh-- done at an impossible rate. Neither Betty nor any of Marcia's other pals would be able to compete with Marcia in her current state. They knew it was best to leave Marcia alone to sort it all out and cross sh-- off her bucket list in her own fashion.

So, the conversation, although somewhat helpful to Marcia, was less than satisfactory, especially since it was punctuated by Betty's sobs. Betty, it seemed, needed a shoulder to cry on even more than Marcia did. Marcia ended up coaxing Betty to bed, telling her that the next day would look brighter after a good night's rest. Marcia even offered to Fed X Betty her sleep mask, for added consolation (polka dots worked similar to cucumbers for soothing eyes). Betty declined. They said good night, with a promise to talk the next day.

Marcia then self-anointed herself with the essential oils Munka had magically recommended for her–lavender to relax and rosemary for focus and concentration. In the weeks ahead, Munka would add peppermint oil to the essential oil mix for added relaxation. Marcia needed all the help she could get when it came to relaxing.

Later that night, Marcia lay in bed, tossing and turning. She looked at the clock. 2:22 flashed back at her in blaring red numbers. Although Marcia had successfully closed her first DISASTER DATE file the previous evening, it had only served to invoke ALL of the DISASTER DATE files lodged in her head. It was obvious that Marcia was not going to be sleeping any time soon. She may as well use her time wisely and attempt to close other DISASTER DATE files.

First on her list was "CRACK HEAD BOB". Bob was the guy who, after their first bowling alley blind date, informed Marcia that he was convinced she was a crack head. A CRACK HEAD, FOR CRYING OUT LOUD! Sure, Marcia was bubbly, and (as Betty phrased it) "intense", especially when she was NERVOUS. But a freaking CRACK HEAD? This seemed like a pretty extreme judgment after only one date with Bob.

Marcia later learned that Bob had been convinced by his Pork Lake, WI bar cronies that she MUST be doing crack to act as psycho as she did on their first date. Bob had, in fact, consulted with a choice group of dating experts to come up with this conclusion…the local BAR FLIES! These guys were all undoubtedly plastered as they formulated THE CRACK HEAD theory. These men obviously did not have much in the way of actual dating experience, although they might know a thing or two about using crack.

Bob had later revealed all of this information to Marcia while sitting in HER hot tub under the stars. And, what was Bob doing at that exact moment? He was hoovering in giant gulps of dope from his one-hitter! Not at ALL ironic or disturbing. (Marcia, of course, was NOT joining him on the one hitter). Wouldn't this qualify as a case of "sweep in front of your own damn doorstep" if there ever was one? Geeeeeez! No wonder Marcia had dumped him when Bob started talking about moving in with her! The guy was a loser.

On a positive note, "Crack Head Bob" HAD provided her with an X-large Carhartt coat that Marcia wore to stave off the -22 temps on her patio while sneaking half-cigarettes.

After her "Crack Head Bob" days, Marcia recalled, her dating game had gone from bad to worse. Marcia had, in effect, started to PAY for bad dates! On an impulse, she joined a Minneapolis dating service called "Date by Debit". Marcia figured if she actually paid for dates, the quality of the date(s) would increase, if not the quantity. As it turned out, Marcia had very unrealistic expectations. In return for large monthly debits to her bank account, Marcia was set up with:

A sweet, spiked-haired biker paper-maker named Rascal. Marcia got a call from Rascal the very day after joining "Date by Debit". When Marcia returned Rascal's call, his answering machine message said, "HELLLLLOOOOO, you've reached Rascal's humble abode…". "OMG," Marcia thought, "Rascal does not sound too promising." She forced herself to follow through on the date they set up that night at nearby Kenny's Chicken House.

Rascal arrived first at Kenny's Chicken House, attired in a faded yellow sleeveless T-shirt. The moment Marcia walked in and spotted Rascal in the sleeveless T, she knew he did not stand a chance. Marcia did not even bother to give the rest of Rascal the once-over. Sleeveless T-shirts were another of Marcia's pet peeves in men's clothing. Marcia could NOT imagine incorporating sleeveless T-shirts into her daily laundry routine.

Instead of being a gentleman and standing up when he saw Marcia, Rascal simply waited for her to approach him. Rascal had succeeded in raising two "red flags" for Marcia–wardrobe issues and no manners - in the first five minutes of their date. Marcia immediately sensed that sleeveless-T Rascal was not the kind of guy who would treat her with the respect she deserved.

Marcia and Rascal had not exactly clicked, either, in terms of alcohol consumption. Rascal sat at the Chicken House bar, drinking an O'Doole's non-alcoholic beer in a frosty mug. He did not once crack a smile. Marcia, overcome with first date "warnings", ended up guzzling margaritas, laughing with other patrons and excusing herself to dance solo by the jukebox when Rascal declined. In other words, making a complete fool of herself–but HAVING FUN! Marcia had no illusions of a second date– Rascal was a deadbeat. Her "Date by Debit" debut, therefore, had not been memorable.

Next, for an exciting change of pace, "Date by Debit" suggested Melvin– an insurance adjuster. Melvin had–unbeknownst to Marcia–abused his insurance software by promptly entering her first name and phone number into the program to get her driving background and profile. Melvin had done this BEFORE he had even called Marcia for the first time. When Marcia's phone rang that evening, Melvin had introduced himself and casually said "Oh, so you drive an '87 Honda Accord and live at 308 7th Avenue North?" Marcia was incredulous! WHO DOES THAT, she thought. WHO USES THEIR WORK SOFTWARE AS A "DATING TOOL?" WASN'T THAT ILLEGAL? Marcia would never abuse the Whisks R Us software in such a fashion. Marcia did not feel this had been a good way for Melvin to "get something started" with her. In fact, Marcia was pissed off at Melvin. Visions of "M & M" monogrammed bath towels vanished in a cloud of vapor.

Now, lying in the dark, Marcia clearly remembered standing in the garage doorway of her "DOLL HOUSE" condo on the sunny summer morning after Melvin had called. She had been sipping cappuccino from her oversized, lime green cappuccino cup (with matching saucer) from Pier One. Reviewing, analyzing, no, processing the invasive phone call from Melvin. As it turned out, Marcia did not have to worry about having to go on an actual date with Melvin. Melvin had never bothered to make the "follow-up" call.

A week later, an apology card from Melvin had arrived in Marcia's mailbox. The card had a droopy-eyed basset hound in a basket on the cover. The contrite text written inside the card contained words that had obviously been "white-ed-out" (painted over with a tiny white-out brush). "WHO DOES THAT?" Marcia thought, "Who uses 'white-out' when composing a short note?" Obviously, Melvin had struggled to figure out what words he could possibly use to make things right.

Marcia had not felt the need to respond to Melvin or his too-little-too-late card. His words smacked of awkward high-school dating notes. She was already resigned to the fact that she and Melvin were not meant to meet.

Melvin, however, had not given up. Melvin sent yet another note to Marcia. Of course, the only reason Melvin could even send notes to Marcia was because he had looked up her freaking address on his software. This note from Melvin had a bit nastier tone. It began with "LOOK Marcia…" ("YIKES," Marcia thought)…and rambled on about how Melvin was on a quest to find the girl of his dreams (that would NOT be Marcia) and how Melvin was not able to talk on the phone as easily as writing note(s). Marcia was confused…didn't Melvin USE THE PHONE to call and tell her he had "looked up her driving profile"?

Marcia had been relieved to cross Melvin off her social "To Do" list. Marcia had been relieved to promptly fire "Date by Debit". Now, alone in her bed, Marcia began to realize that maybe being single and lonely was not such a bad thing, after all.

Marcia sighed in frustration and looked again at the clock… it was 4:44 A.M. On an impulse, she decided to use her self-imposed clock rule and make a silent wish to the 4:44 spirits. Marcia had just spent two hours and twenty-two minutes of her beauty rest reliving unsuccessful dates. Her wish was simply to PURGE HERSELF OF "DISASTER DATE" FILES ONCE AND FOR ALL! SHE WAS SO OVER IT. SO OVER THE DATING THANG. SHE HAD JUST HAD IT. UP TO HER OVER-WHISKED SCALP. FORGET DATING. MARCIA WAS DONE. FIN. NOT ONE DATE "GOT HER". AND SHE WAS SKEPTICAL THAT A FUTURE DATE EVER WOULD.

After all, it had only been … what? Fifteen freaking years of failed attempts, fifteen freaking years of trying, over and over again. Of staying optimistic, thinking positive, jumping back on that dang small-town horse, hoping upon hope that just ONE FREAKING MALE IN THE UNIVERSE WOULD GET HER.

Yet even while Marcia was having these futile thoughts, a teeny, tiny voice inside her head was assuring her that she was not really DONE-DONE. Marcia laughed outright at this thought. Tonight, Marcia had just needed a good "DISASTER DATE" cleansing. It didn't mean that she would never try again. Marcia, in her heart, still had hope that she would someday find her BOY-FOR-ALL-SEASONS. The important thing now was to erase the "date history clutter" from her head. She just needed to stay positive. Marcia pressed her thumbs together for German good luck and, feeling lighter than she had in a long time, promptly sank into a deep, dreamless sleep.

JANUARY 11–SUNDAY
DAYS TILL MUSIC CRUISE = 63
MARCIA'S BEVVIES-OF-THE-MOMENT=MARCIA HAS RESORTED TO HER "BOTTLES" - LAVENDER OIL (TO CALM HER), ROSEMARY (TO FOCUS) AND THE FREAKING BOTTLE OF BAILEY'S (TO SELF MEDICATE)
BRANDI'S LYRICS (VIA HEADPHONES) THAT GET HER THRU=IN A CROWDED ROOM, I'M ALONE

"…and where the hell did the heat go," Marcia thought the next morning, taking deep yoga breaths while applying lavender oil to calm herself. Marcia wrapped her 8-foot self-knit scarf more tightly around her neck and adjusted her fleece Cayamo blankie. The furnace had not kicked in for several hours. The thermostat now registered a chilly fifty-nine degrees. Marcia's weekend was not starting off in a warm and fuzzy manner.

While shivering and sipping a warm cup of hot chocolate, Marcia opened the Haystack County News to read about the biggest meth bust in the history of Haystack County. Ironically, Marcia's finely-tuned editorial eye moved instead to a snippet in the Haystack County police blotter. It read: "THEFT OF A FURNACE FROM A FORECLOSED HOME IN HAYSTACK TWP REPORTED".

Hmmmmm, Marcia mused, this (like jumping off the bridge into the Rum River) might be worth considering. The police blotter estimated the furnace loss at $3,000. Marcia KNEW her current bank balance would not cover a new $3,000 furnace. Her current bank balance would not even cover a $300 service call! Marcia doubted that even a (dreaded) trip to Menards would be enough to fix her broken furnace. She stubbornly refused to call a repair person–weekend rates were hideous! Marcia's only option was to locate her owner's manual and try to fix the damn thing herself (not one of her strengths, mechanical stuff). Why hadn't she sent back the Service Plus enrollment card when she had the chance? It, like her SAMS Club Rewards check, had disappeared from her kitchen counter. Marcia assumed both of these items were now lying in a bed of dust balls under the fridge. She absolutely REFUSED to add moving out the fridge to the Marcia-To-Do-List (M-T-D-L) on a freaking Sunday! Moving appliances would TOTALLY offset her massage therapy, for crying out loud!

How then, Marcia mused, could she possibly pull off the theft of a new furnace? Marcia picked up the Haystack County News to re-read the police blotter. Re-reading the item sparked her imagination. It was Halloween the very next night. She and Betty could dress up as thieves, no; wait… she and Betty could dress up as Spy vs. Spy for Halloween. While in full costume (one black spy, one white spy; Betty would probably choose to be the black spy), they would casually snag a new furnace from one of the many foreclosed Haystack homes. Betty was extremely handy with tools—she had installed a new furnace at her farmhouse the previous year. If anyone stopped them while in possession of said furnace, Marcia and Betty could tell them they were setting up to film "THE WHITE SPY (MARCIA) dropping a furnace on THE BLACK SPY (BETTY)" for an upcoming major motion picture. People in Wisconsin always fell for that kind of local drama. It was a brilliant idea!

THE FREAKIN' FURNACE PROBLEM IS SOLVED, thought Marcia, and with a sigh, she mentally checked it off of the M-T-D-L. She then peeled off her long underwear and began to primp for a hasty retreat to the warmth of the "Grindin' Gossip" coffee shop.

JANUARY 11–SUNDAY (CONTINUED)
DAYS TILL MUSIC CRUISE = 63
MARCIA'S BEVVIE-OF-THE-MOMENT=WEAK, SUBSTANDARD "GRINDIN' GOSSIP" COFFEE SERVED IN A CHIPPED GREEN JOHN DEERE LOGO MUG
BRANDI'S LYRICS (VIA HEADPHONES) THAT GET HER THRU=I'M HAPPY CAN'T YOU SEE, I'M ALRIGHT

A short time later, Marcia relaxed in a cozy booth at the "Grindin' Gossip" with her friend, Mary. They had just been served large cups of steaming coffee and raspberry white chocolate scones, still warm from the oven. Mary had very exciting news to share with Marcia. An "out-of-the-freaking-blue" blind date prospect had magically materialized for Marcia. Mary's beau of thirteen years, Henry, had finagled a date for Marcia with his cousin, Farmer Tony. Farmer Tony (aka "FT"), was a well-known celebrity of sorts who lived in nearby Grazel Grove. Mary could not emphasize enough how fortunate Marcia was to be offered such an opportunity.

Marcia had heard talk of Farmer Tony (FT) thru local gossip at the "Grindin' Grounds" coffee shop in Haystack. The "Grindin' Grounds" coffee shop was nicknamed the "Grindin' Gossip" coffee shop by those "in the know". As in "grind out" the gossip. ANY or ALL IMPORTANT LOCAL INFO COULD BE GLEANED just by stopping at the "G.G." for a cup of Joe.

Marcia was already aware that Farmer Tony was no small cheese in Grazel Grove. He was probably the most eligible bachelor in West-Central WI. Not only was FT a dairy farmer; he also grew hazel nuts on the side. Even though Grazel Grove was within commuting distance of Haystack (an easy 45 minutes), Marcia and FT had not yet crossed paths. This was probably due to the fact that Marcia was on the road so much lately, "repping" scalp whisks.

Over the next three caffeine-fueled hours, Marcia learned (via Mary) exactly why FT was considered such a great catch:

PERTINENT FT FACTS (PRE-BLIND DATE WITH MARCIA):

1. FT WAS RICH. FT was the MAIN SOURCE OF WOOD FOR STATE OF WI SIGN POSTS. He managed 88 acres of old-growth HAZEL NUT trees. He oversaw a herd of 400 dairy cows. He had 14 full-time employees. FT also sold cheese and

hazel nuts in 16 states, MN being one of them. It was one heck of a large-scale operation. FT's uncle and brother-in-law were also local farmers. As FT phrased it, "We all help each other out. But we don't share checkbooks, if you know what I mean."

2. FT HAD A GORGEOUS NEW 4,100 SQF FARM HOUSE. The down-side of this was the home's décor (described in horrifying detail by Mary, who had gotten a peek at his photo albums). FT's home décor consisted of multi-hued-red shag carpeting and olive green appliances, which were custom-ordered 70's-style recreations. Olive green accents in the bathroom were used to "tie it all together". However, if Marcia could only "make it work" with FT, she could REDECORATE the entire freaking farmhouse! (FT obviously did NOT need to know this at such an early stage, PRE-DATE). Marcia had already decided her goal was to "SPEND NEXT XMAS ON THE FARM" (she credited her mom for this excellent idea).

3. FT HAD A RETAIL CHEESE SHOP ON THE PREMISES. Marcia was already envisioning becoming the cheese shop manager. The shop could be used as a retail outlet for her scalp whisks. And, best of all, she could then "telecommute", which meant no winter travel on nasty, icy WI back roads. Marcia could even sell her blockbuster novel (aka screenplay) in the cheese shop, if she ended up self-publishing. THIS WAS A BRILLIANT IDEA! BRILLIANT!

4. FT WAS NOT HALF BAD LOOKING. Although Marcia would not go as far as saying he rated an "EASY ON THE EYES" award. Even as seen through her botched Rx glasses. FT was prematurely balding and had a bit of a "paunch" but Marcia was confident she could overlook these flaws because FT had so many other redeeming qualities.

5. FT WAS LOOKING FOR A WIFE - OF THE OPPOSITE SEX/FEMALE PERSUASION - WHO COULD COOK AND CLEAN. Marcia was a bit nervous about this fact, because she fell into a more husband-like classification. Marcia was the lone bread winner of her family, performing a job that sucked the life

out of her. She had no energy—nothing left to give—when it came to dinnertime. Or house cleaning.

6. FT LIKED TO DISCO AND SING KAROKE EVERY SATURDAY NIGHT AT THE "THIRSTY THERMALS TAP". The "THIRSTY THERMALS TAP" was an 80's-themed disco club with a weekend DJ. FT religiously met up there with his "500 card club cronies" and their wives every Saturday night. FT's casual "TT TAP" attire consisted of: two-toned denim jeans accented with a large rodeo-style belt buckle; a starched white button-down; a cow-shaped bolo string tie and soft grey leather cowboy boots. FT would spend the night dancing with his pals' wives. FT was known to drink a bit too much on Saturday nights; he usually had to switch to 7Up at 11:00 P.M.

7. FT OWNED A COMPLETE COLLECTION OF CAST-IRON GREEN, YELLOW AND RED MINI-JOHN DEERE TRACTORS AND COMBINES. COVETED BY MANY WEST CENTRAL WISCONSIN FARMERS AND THEIR WIVES. WORTH A BUNDLE. IN MINT CONDITION. Marcia, being a collector herself, honed right in on the prospect of sharing this particular personal property of FT's.

8. FT WORE FARMER GLASSES FOR NIGHT DRIVING IN WISCONSIN SNOWSTORMS. THIS MEANT FT AND MARCIA SHARED SOMETHING IN COMMON RIGHT OFF THE BAT - BOTH WORE DORKY GLASSES. Marcia discovered (from the photo Mary provided) that FT actually looked kinda cute in his dorky glasses.

Marcia could not help but be intrigued by the deluge of information that Mary provided her with over "Grindin' Grounds" coffee that day. Marcia was simply adhering to one of her dad's favorite expressions: "GET THE FACTS". Marcia now had several pertinent "FT FACTS". She and Mary decided it would behoove them to spend more time doing a "comparison study" of sorts between "FT FACTS" and "MARCIA FACTS". That way they could gage whether the date would be a success before it even took place. This was a common practice developed by Marcia and used by many of her female friends, especially when it came to wealthy, eligible bachelors.

PERTINENT MARCIA FACTS (PRE-BLIND DATE WITH FT):

1. MARCIA WAS POOR; OR, AT BEST, WORKING MIDDLE CLASS.

2. MARCIA HAD A DAINTY BUT WORN, 812 SQF "DOLL HOUSE" CONDO: Marcia's boss had seen her whisk sales potential and loaned her 3k for the down payment. The condo had previously been owned by a sweet eighty-year-old widow, who was forced to sell it after falling down the treacherous basement stairs. The widow's son had moved her to a retirement home. Marcia had always felt horrible about this.

   Because the tiny condo had once been home to a family of four, Marcia had felt confident she could make it work for her and her young daughter. The back yard was three times the size of the actual condo. The driveway was lined with 100' Norway pine trees. Marcia was able to do her whisk sales job at a large desk set up in her kitchen (it was no wonder Marcia had trouble cooking meals). "DOLL HOUSE" was, overall, a godsend. While waiting to hear if she had gotten the home loan, Marcia had stood in the driveway, with tears rolling down her cheeks, silently pleading with Munka. "Please, Munka", Marcia thought, "Please kick in your special guardian angel powers to help us get the home loan approved." And Munka, as always, had done her duty.

3. MARCIA SOLD GOURMET FOOD ON THE SIDE TO SUPPLEMENT HER INCOME.
   Marcia had several jobs. Marcia sold scalp massaging whisks. Marcia was a single parent. Marcia also designed "themed" gift baskets (Tex-Mex, Hula girl, etc.) filled with gourmet food. Marcia sold these baskets to a home builder; in fact, was responsible for delivering them to new homeowners when they purchased a home. In return, Marcia received cold, hard cash. Marcia's extra gift basket income provided Marcia and Daughter with "fun money", for nights out on the town or for stuffed animals. Or

other necessities such as massages, or artist supplies (black pens and copier paper) for Daughter.

Marcia was especially proud of the fact that Daughter created sketches of Marcia, getting out of the tub, when Daughter was only four years old. Daughter, at age four, already appreciated the nude human form as art. Daughter's sketches, at age four, looked like professional abstract art. Therefore, Marcia always found creative ways to finance art supplies for her gifted Daughter.

4. MARCIA WAS NOT HALF-BAD LOOKING. SOME WOULD SAY "CUTE".
Her big brown eyes were her best feature. Her somewhat-yoga-toned bod was not bad for a fifty year-old–people were often surprised when she revealed her age. Also, her smile could light up a room (well, HER room anyway). Marcia could, when encouraged, be a fashion plate, constantly updating her wardrobe as dollars allowed. She could still get away with wearing "younger" cotton dresses with sandals. Marcia was a GREAT CATCH, if given half a chance (not immediately written off as a lunatic "Crack Head").

5. MARCIA, TOO, WAS LOOKING FOR A "WIFE" - OF THE OPPOSITE SEX/MALE PERSUASION - WHO COULD COOK AND CLEAN.
Marcia currently had a "Back Home" Styrofoam cooler at her side door. This equated to a fully prepped meal delivered each night to her doorstep. Versus the alternative; actually cooking MN wild rice soup from scratch for her and Daughter. Or steak and potatoes and FRESH VEGETABLES. Marcia justified her "meal-delivery" expense with her supplemental income and because of the fact that she had no time to PLAN AND/OR DELIVER HOME COOKED MEALS AT DOLL HOUSE.

6. MARCIA WAS A FORMER DJ WHO LIVED AND BREATHED ALTERNATIVE MUSIC.
Marcia's musical taste was an anomaly in Haystack, WI. Marcia would definitely have a hard time acclimating to disco at the "THIRSTY THERMALS TAP" on Saturday nights. Marcia

would much rather spend her Saturday nights at an alternative music venue in Minneapolis or Chicago.

7. MARCIA OWNED NUMEROUS COMPLETE COLLECTIONS, MOSTLY FAMILY MOMENTOS.
Marcia's most treasured possessions were those that had been inherited from relatives who were now part of Marcia's ancestral spirit support system. These included orange crate ends; real-gold trimmed, Homer Laughlin Georgian Eggshell flower-pattern china (made in the U.S.A.); display cases full of miniature pencils and perfume vials; mirrors so old she could see the brush strokes of chemical used to create the "glass"; crystal wine and sherbet glasses; a "cow-jumped-over-the-moon" antique cookie jar; and ornate picture frames hand-picked with her dad from her great-uncle Hank's "shop" that was originally the family home (some of these frames hung empty on their DOLL HOUSE walls. For some reason, this really bugged Betty). Marcia had even hand-painted one of Hank's old medicine chests and filled it with miniatures she had collected on her travels abroad.

8. MARCIA WORE BOTCHED HALF NEAR-SIGHTED, HALF BI-FOCAL "OLD LADY" GLASSES FOR NIGHT DRIVING IN WI SNOWSTORMS.
FT and Marcia would both be wearing dorky glasses on their blind date. Marcia also looked kinda cute in her glasses – she had been told that she looked like a librarian in them.

9. MARCIA, IN HER USUAL OPTIMISTIC MODE, HAD ALREADY TOLD HER BOSS TO GET THE MODEM HOOKED UP ON "THE FARM".
Unfortunately, the modem to the farm would be incurring long distance phone charges at day rates (both Haystack and Grazel Grove were a bit behind on hi-speed technology).

Regrettably, in matters of the heart, Marcia was known for sometimes OVERLOOKING AND/OR SKEWING THE FACTS, even after doing a "comparison study". Marcia's wild imagination and over-analytical mind would often have a first date "love story" written before she even met the man! Marcia was such a romantic, optimistic, heart-on-her-sleeve woman that she visualized a BOY-FOR-ALL-SEASONS each and every time she accepted a date. Marcia vowed to Mary that this time she would try to keep an open mind and not write the usual passionate love story script in her head beforehand. That way, Marcia could avoid a potential letdown.

Once they had sufficiently prepped Marcia for her date with FT, Mary and Marcia parted ways, with the promise that Mary would be the first to know how the blind date with FT turned out. Marcia was feeling "cautiously optimistic" about her upcoming date.

JANUARY 16–FRIDAY
DAYS TILL MUSIC CRUISE = 58
MARCIA'S BEVVIE-OF-THE-MOMENT=BAILEY'S ON THE ROCKS THE SIZE OF EAST TEXAS
BRANDI'S LYRICS (VIA HEADPHONES) THAT GET HER THRU=YOU CAN'T BREAK A HEART THAT WASN'T EVEN YOURS TO BREAK

The following Friday, Marcia returned home after her steakhouse blind date with FT. Choking back tears, she powered up her laptop and immediately began to write as a way to process exactly what had transpired that night:

MARCIA'S CONCLUSIONS (POST-DATE WITH FT):

1. MUTUAL LIKES:
   Both FT and Marcia liked microwave popcorn and M & M's (FT loved green ones, natch; Marcia preferred the Peanut Butter variety); PHOTO ALBUMS (although Marcia did not KEEP HER PHOTO ALBUMS WITH HER AT ALL TIMES LIKE FT); and CLEAN HOUSES (Marcia cheated by hiring Merry Maids).

2. MUTUAL INTERESTS: NONE.

3. FT DID NOT KNOW HOW TO USE A LAPTOP. MARCIA WAS A WHIZ.

4. MARCIA DID NOT KNOW HOW TO USE A COMBINE. FT WAS A WHIZ.

5. FT DID NOT LIKE READING OR KNOW HOW TO ENJOY A NOVEL. MARCIA DEVOURED GOOD NOVELS.

6. FT DID NOT LIKE GIVING HUGS ("WE'RE NOT A HUGGING KIND OF A FAMILY"). MARCIA RELIED ON GETTING (AND GIVING) HUGS.

7. FT COULD GO FOR TWO STRAIGHT DAYS WITHOUT SLEEP (DURING THE HEIGHT OF HAZEL NUT SEASON).

Marcia relied on a mandatory power nap schedule (20 minutes every day at lunchtime, if possible, and then she was good for another 10 hours).

8. FT ENJOYED BEING SERVED LUNCH WHILE ON HIS TOP-OF-THE-LINE COMBINE.

Marcia could not imagine serving combine lunches. Marcia's server days had been over since age 21, when she quit waitressing at the Dairy Mart. NOTE: Daughter was the sole exception to this rule.

9. FT EXPECTED TO BE SERVED HOME-COOKED DINNERS AS WELL.

FT had grilled Marcia on her cooking skills. FT had wanted DETAILS, such as can you make lasagna? (Marcia's response: I most certainly can, as she envisioned popping the Stouffer's into the oven). FT wanted to know if Marcia was a "meat and potatoes" kind of gal (Marcia's response: well, we really like cheese). FT's weekly cooking repertoire included tater-tot hot dish (a western Wisconsin staple), fish, pizza, pork chops, and, of course, steak and potatoes. Fried potatoes. Fried in a black cast-iron skillet that had been in the FT family for generations. It was obvious to Marcia that FT could easily kick her butt in the cooking department. But it wasn't a fair comparison because FT was able to set his own schedule on the farm.

10. MARCIA'S HAIR WAS ALMOST AS SHORT AS FT'S.

FT initially told Marcia that her hair looked nice. After a few vodka tonics, however, FT modified his compliment and told Marcia that her hair was too short.

11. FT USED A BLIND DATE AS A POTENTIAL GENETIC (REPRODUCTION) FACT-FINDING MISSION.

Marcia was so appalled by this first-date behavior that she had consumed four Chivas-scotch-on-the-rocks, which was very unlike her. Marcia was usually on her best alcohol consumption behavior on blind dates.

12. FT'S "MARRIAGE QUESTIONAIRRE" INCLUDED 40 PLUS OBSERVATIONS AND/OR RANDOM QUESTIONS FOR MARCIA.

FT commented on the condition of her teeth (FT: YOUR TEETH LOOK PRETTY GOOD); the quality of Marcia's hair (FT: YOUR HAIR IS REALLY THICK, ISN'T IT?) and the size of her ears (FT: YOU REALLY HAVE PETITE EARS, DO SMALL EARS RUN IN YOUR FAMILY?). Marcia did her best to remain polite and answer FT's questions, while squirming uncomfortably in her chair. Secretly, she was beginning to feel as though she were trying out for a local beauty queen contest. It was becoming apparent to Marcia that FT was one "piece of work".

When FT began to question Marcia about her family's health history (FT: HOW OLD WERE YOUR GRANDPARENTS WHEN THEY DIED?), Marcia was able to silence him with the response that her grandma had died of ovarian cancer when she was 45. This really threw FT off. He promptly ordered another vodka tonic and changed the subject to the upcoming Twins baseball season.

After consuming excessive scotch while being interrogated by FT, Marcia could not even fathom what sleeping with Farmer Tony would be like. Nor could Marcia imagine what PROCREATING with FT would be like. Sleeping together would be a scientific experiment; "reproduction appointments" would be set up on select days of the month. On all other days of the month, Marcia would be starved for affection. Marcia's heart slowly began to sink with disappointment. The farmhouse Xmas ornament her mom had sent to her for good luck on her blind date with FT had not helped one bit. Marcia was, in FT's eyes, just a potential combine sandwich-delivery cow. Marcia knew she would never be happy in this role.

FT'S CONCLUSIONS (POST-DATE WITH MARCIA):
(Marcia heard FT's date recap to his cousin Henry second-hand from Mary)

FT TO HENRY: "IF THAT MARCIA GAL IS INVITED TO YOUR WEDDING, I AM NOT SHOWING UP! SHE IS PSYCHO! SHE WORKS WITH THOSE FREAKY COMPUTER THINGS. SHE IS NOT GOOD WIFE MATERIAL! SHE ACTED LIKE A HUSBAND/BREADWINNER ON OUR DATE! PLEASE, HENRY, DO ME A FAVOR AND DON'T SET ME UP ON ANY OTHER BLIND DATES!"

MARCIA'S RESPONSE (TO SELF) RE: FT:
So much pain and no gain. Marcia would rather be alone in her DOLL HOUSE condo than stuck in an eight-foot GRAZEL GROVE, WI snowdrift, "alone" because "her man" was unable to communicate, only plant seeds.

And when it came right down to it, Marcia had only wanted to marry FT in order to become joint owner of the mini-John Deere tractor collection. And play her favorite card game "500". And manage the retail cheese shop.

Ulterior motives for getting into a relationship were never a good sign. Marsha realized she had gotten her priorities all screwed up. Farmer Tony was not BOY-FOR-ALL-SEASONS material nor was he even BOY-FOR-THE-WINTER material. Farmer Tony, instead, would be an easy DISASTER DATE for Marcia to cleanse from her heart. She would probably not go on another blind date FOR AT LEAST 3, MAYBE EVEN 6 MONTHS! "XMAS ON THE FARM", it seemed, WAS NOT MEANT TO BE.

JANUARY 22–THURSDAY
DAYS TILL MUSIC CRUISE = 52
MARCIA'S BEVVIE-OF-THE-MOMENT=POMEGRANATE WINE SERVED IN AN HEIRLOOM WINE GLASS
BRANDI'S LYRICS (VIA HEADPHONES) THAT GET HER THRU=IN A CROWDED ROOM, I'M ALONE

Times were hard in Haystack, WI. New home sale gift basket orders were at an all-time low. Whisk scalp sales were also suffering. Marcia's dual-job income had been reduced to a mere pittance. She was not inspired to work on her blockbuster novel aka screenplay; her dire cash flow situation was all-consuming. It was minus twenty-six degrees below on a lonely winter night. The furnace had still not been repaired–Marcia was relying solely on her gas oven to keep the DOLL HOUSE pipes from freezing.

Marcia had already spent the entire freaking day preparing the next weeks' batch of knödels since she was down to only potatoes and flour in the pantry. She still wasn't sure if she had perfected the knödel recipe (the ratio of flour to potato) as expertly as her mom. Marcia sighed–she would probably never get the ratio right, no matter how many batches of knödels she made. Hopefully, the extra dumplings she planned on freezing would not thaw into pasty blobs and be inedible. At this point, every meal counted. She tried to be optimistic; in fact, she had splurged and purchased both butter AND bacon to top tonight's knödel dinner. There was no sense in worrying too much about her cholesterol level at this point. She poured more pomegranate wine into her heirloom wine glass and comforted herself with the fact that at least her liquor cabinet was still full.

Marcia was devoting the night to brainstorming potential income-earning opportunities. Her imagination had been sparked by an idea on her last trip to the Hurricane "self-serve" car wash. She thought it might be fiscally beneficial to try out a "dollar ponzi scheme" of sorts on the kind, 65-plus gentlemen who frequented the car wash.

Marcia's plan worked as such: Marcia would stand at the car wash dollar bill changer. When an older gent approached the bill changer, she would ask if he could assist her by exchanging her dollar bill with the corner ripped off for a "whole" dollar bill that would work properly in the bill changer. This, along with her dazzling smile, would be a convincing enough "Opening

Line" to somehow charm the elderly man out of additional dollars from his fat wallet as well ($1's, $5's, $10's, $20's…even $100's were not out of the question). If nothing else, Marcia could potentially earn at least ONE buck by distracting the man enough to make him forget to take her ripped dollar bill.

Marcia had to first somehow CHARM one of her "car wash prospects" into forfeiting his brand-spanking-new snowmobile trailer for her "operation". That way, she could run her "dollar ponzi scheme" right in the car wash parking lot, using the trailer as a "base camp" to avoid the WI wind chills. Marcia was confident that she could pull this off.

The "dollar ponzi scheme" system would be much less humiliating than, say, actually using her BODY as a means to generate cash from the forfeited snowmobile trailer. A "hooker scheme" would involve moving the entire "operation" inside the car wash so as not to create suspicion. Just the mere thought of the over-sized hydraulic car wash door opening to admit her next "JOHN" was more than Marcia could possibly bear. She imagined that, on any given day, her "range" of clientele would be freaky and disturbing, to say the least.

Along this same vein, Marcia was convinced she could simplify the whole car wash "hooker scheme" by advertising her wares right out on Haystack County Road 4! Marcia would probably choose to hang out near Summerblue's, the only "upscale" bar and restaurant in town. She would have to be sure to stay out of range of the nearby Haystack cop shop, which bustled with activity 24/7.

One of Haystack's many police officers constantly patrolled County Road 4 in a sparkling new white Ford F150 pickup, accented with the bright blue "Haystack Police Department" logo. On the back of the truck, the message, "This vehicle was seized from a drunk driver arrest" was painted in large black letters. Marcia had no problem supporting this method of advertising. Marcia was all about "forfeited property". As long as the F150 did not interfere with her well laid-out plan to set up her "hooker scheme".

RANDOM THOUGHT: based on the -32 degree temps, Marcia may have to wear her daughter's rainbow-striped legwarmers. Not ONLY the legwarmers, mind you. Marcia was not sure that legwarmers, even rainbow-striped legwarmers, would help generate record amounts of business on County Road 4.

Marcia sighed and got up to pour herself more pomegranate wine. Although she was attempting to put on a brave front, she knew, in her heart, that she would never aspire to become the small-town "snowmobile trailer hooker". She would never be able to "work it" from the Summerblue parking lot. Granted, the pay would be spectacular but Marcia would never forgive herself for sacrificing her self-respect. Marcia would rather pawn her silver Mercury dimes at record high prices than pawn herself off on strange men. She needed to put any "hooker scheme" thoughts to bed. In fact, she needed to ditch her "dollar ponzi scheme" idea as well. Marcia knew herself well enough to know that she would definitely lose sleep over even one stolen car wash dollar from a helpful gentleman. Marcia would have to come up with an alternative plan to generate income—such as selling homemade baked goods (smorkranz and rice krispie bars) out of her back door. After all, everyone in town knew that Marcia's baking skills were unsurpassed in Haystack.

JANUARY 25–SUNDAY
DAYS TILL MUSIC CRUISE = 49
M'S BEVVIE-OF-THE-MOMENT=CHEAP "HOUSE" RED WINE AT J & J'S AND WEAK, SUBSTANDARD "COVERED BRIDGE CAFÉ" COFFEE SERVED IN A STAINED BROWN PLASTIC MUG
BRANDI'S LYRICS (VIA HEADPHONES) THAT GET HER THRU=I'M HAPPY CAN'T YOU SEE, I'M ALRIGHT

Marcia's phone was currently beeping while on a call with Betty. Her Caller ID told Marcia to take it because it was a call from Loony Lake, WI! Marcia was very excited to see the "715" area code. She deduced it was a call from Irish Bun, the man she had gone on a blind date with two nights earlier at J & J's annual Wild Game Feed & Gun Raffle. Marcia's resolve NOT TO GO ON ANOTHER BLIND DATE FOR AT LEAST 3, MAYBE EVEN 6 MONTHS had lasted exactly ONE WEEK! Rufus had come through and snagged Marcia the elite "Game Feed" date with Irish, simply because Irish was desperate not to attend the event without a beautiful woman on his burly arm. Marcia promptly cut Betty off and clicked over to the call.

The phone conversation with Irish began with a recap of their Friday night Wild Game Feed date. The date had seemed like a success - Irish Bun had snuck out Marcia's front door at sunrise. Irish Bun told Marcia that she needed to oil her squeaky front door - he had tried to be soooo careful exiting, so as not to awake her. Marcia asked Irish Bun why he didn't oil the door as he snuck out ("didn't you see the job jar?"). That got a laugh out of Irish.

Irish said his dog was waiting for him when he got home at 7:30 A.M Saturday morning. Irish also said he was going to leave a note for Marcia but that he didn't want to go through her drawers (so to speak). Marcia told him he could go through her drawers, just not all of her drawers. "Cuuuuute," Marcia thought, "a note from a man - that was sexy." Marcia would have used her skills to edit the note for proper punctuation and spelling. Marcia was smart enough to ask Irish what the note would have said. Irish replied "thanks for the sleep over, I had a good time, and maybe we could do it again".

The Wild Game Feed & Gun Raffle at J & J's the previous night had been a blast. J & J's, being a third-generation business, was packed to the gills with families in matching yellow and black snowmobile attire, lone bachelors in black and white Stetson hats, and sixtyish farmers flirting with young women in florescent Victoria Secret sweatpants. One or two of these women had already bore the farmers' children.

The only challenge at "the feed" was that Marcia had to ingest samples of roasted rabbit and pheasant and mallard duck and grouse and squirrel and venison and Canadian geese from the buffet in order to make a good first impression on Irish Bun. Marcia had to conjure up a fake smile as she gagged on her bite of pinkish squirrel flesh. The buffet had also included an assortment of hot dishes, including chow mien hot dish, spaghetti hot dish, tater-tot hot dish and lima bean hot dish. Desert consisted of a Wisconsin specialty–deep dish apple pie with melted cheese on top - and plate after plate of bars: seven-layer bars, lemon bars dusted with powdered sugar, carrot bars with cream cheese frosting and blondies. The liquor flowed freely, especially bourbon and Coors Lite. There was a DJ spinning country music and the dance floor was packed all night. Marcia and Irish had danced to two songs; however, Marcia was unable to pretend she knew how to dance "country", which got Irish a bit frustrated. Irish was all about country.

The "feed" ended abruptly when one of the young women in sweatpants hurled on the dance floor after too many free shots of tequila. Marcia was secretly amused and relieved about this–she could only stand so much "feed and country". It was all such a contrast to the urban club scene in Minneapolis.

Afterwards, Irish, being the perfect gentleman, took Marcia out to coffee en route to Haystack at the "Covered Bridge Café", an all-night diner built under an actual covered bridge. Marcia and Irish rehashed the evening while sipping watery coffee and staring out at the frozen banks of the Spirit River. There were only a few awkward moments in their conversation, which Marcia saw as a good sign.

Once Marcia and Irish got back to Marcia's condo, a heavy make-out session ensued, courtesy of massive amounts of Coors Lite on Irish's part and an additional glass of no-longer-cheap red wine on Marcia's part.

Marcia was a bit disappointed in the QUALITY of Irish's kisses but decided that it was better than being gummed to death by a toothless shark at midnight. Irish's tongue was more insistent and less well-aimed than Marcia was used to. Nonetheless, it was fun to actually be kissing a man. Marcia had felt a little rusty at kissing herself.

Now Marcia continued to chat with Irish about how his Saturday had been … he said he was tired but "on a high". He had been in his garage working on his car for the upcoming racing season. He had taken a break to grill burgers with his sons (ages 11 and 12? - Marcia was not sure she had that right). Irish had just now checked his messages and found two—one from his brother and one from Marcia.

Marcia told Irish about how she had run on no sleep again the previous day. She relayed how her sister and brother-in-law had stopped by for a visit. That she had been able to take a power nap after the visit to recover from "up all night Friday". Irish told her he was thinking about calling her on Saturday but thought he might've "taken a lot outta Marcia" on Friday night. Marcia thought Irish was very cute and sweet, even if his kissing was lacking in passion and substance. Passionless kisses did not necessarily bode well for a second date…or the bedroom.

Of course, then Marcia had to push the envelope and say the "I want to mail you baked goods" thang. Marcia was ALWAYS baking for potential second dates. Marcia spent hours of her free time recreating old-world family recipes—smorkranz, chocolate oatmeal chunk cookies, sour cream cookies, ranger cookies, date filled cookies—and wrapping them in cute tissue paper or Tupperware with pink curled ribbons and shipping them off to prospective dates. Marcia NEVER got any care packages in return from said prospective dates. And what hurt Marcia the most was that sometimes the cookies that she lovingly sent sat on the guy's kitchen counter and got stale. What a waste of Marcia's time and energy. Not to mention the expense of jumbo sized Hershey's bars, butter, flour, etc.

Marcia then switched conversational gears and asked Irish if she was banned from Loony Lake because she had dissed it, geographically. Irish reassured her that no, Marcia was not prohibited from visiting Loony Lake.

Irish went on to say that maybe Marcia could come up north for a visit. Marcia gave Irish not one, but two "outs" on his invite. First she hinted that Irish might have to work on his race car in order to get it done for the opening day car show at the race track. Irish said no, he did not have to work on his car ALL weekend. Second, Marcia hinted that, given his busy schedule, Irish would probably have to wait to see her until after she went on the music cruise. Again, Irish said no, he did not think he could wait that long to see her. Once Marcia was thus reassured, she and Irish discussed their respective schedules. Irish then gave Marcia directions to his house. Marcia told Irish, that, using his directions, she would probably make a left-hand turn at Fort Lager instead of a right turn and end up at boot camp. Mutual laughter ensued.

Marcia then decided to go for broke and asked Irish if he would be up to entertaining her the following weekend. Irish said he thought he could handle that task. ("OMG!" Marcia thought, "It looks as though I might be closing in on ANOTHER date with Irish!" Marcia almost NEVER got a second date!). Irish told Marcia that "we could have apple pie". Marcia said, "no, cuz after one slice I'd be hitting the pillow and I would miss out on the rest of the up-north evening." Marcia told Irish that if he wanted to please her, he could have a few Mike's Hard Lemonades on ice. Marcia was, if nothing else, a cheap date.

Later that day, Marcia put on Martin Zellar as background music to comfort her. Irish actually knew who Martin Zellar was. Irish also knew who the Murderous Lilac Bushes were—in fact, Irish knew the band members on a personal level. Marcia plopped down in her massage-with heat-aerodynamic chair with her laptop Granny and reflected on (READ: over-analyzed) her phone conversation with Irish. Marcia was very scared. Marcia was scared because she wondered if Irish had gotten the same first impression that most of her other first dates had gotten—that Marcia was a crazy woman.

After all, Marcia HAD told Irish about how she was "processing" their first date at her Granny keyboard. Marcia HAD gone on to tell Irish that he WAS NOW IN HER BLOCKBUSTER NOVEL AKA SCREENPLAY-IN-PROGRESS but that Irish should be flattered by this because Marcia had started a NEW chapter just for him. Marcia had started a fresh new chapter after four long years because she was harboring hope that Irish would become her new BOY-FOR-THE-WINTER.

But did Marcia stop there with Irish? Noooooo…Marcia had gone on to say that all names in "the novel" had been changed to protect the innocent. That there were, of course, no incriminating details about Irish in the book (both Marcia and Irish had snickered at this information). That the new chapter was only Marcia's "perspective" from their first date together. Marcia STUPIDLY went on to add that she didn't have a photo of Irish to scan for the opening page of the "Irish Bun" chapter like she did for the "STD" chapter.

"OMG," Marcia suddenly thought, "I am a total basket case and I'd better SHUT UP before I blow my chances for a second date." This was all TMI (Too Much Information) for Irish. Too much information too soon ALWAYS got Marcia in trouble and kept Marcia home alone on a consistent basis.

The TMI concept also applied to Marcia's gal pals. Marcia vowed not to disclose ANY details of her Irish Bun date with ANY of her friends. Certainly not Rufus, who had been responsible for setting up the blind date. Certainly not her next door neighbor, Alicia, who lived safely in sin with her beau—boring, steady, consistent Ben—and whom Marcia secretly believed thrived on Marcia's dating misfortunes. Marcia was not going to talk to ANYONE about her date. Marcia would ONLY talk to Irish. Marcia would learn to confide in ONLY the good, strong man that was Irish. Marcia would begin, for once, to foster a healthy relationship with a male. Marcia did, after all, have a good shot at a second date with Irish! Everyone else in the entire neighborhood (and surrounding community) would be cut off from Marcia's latest dating gossip from this point forward. Everyone else got date gossip "pink slips" (and not the kind she wore to work)!

Marcia made a mental note to impress upon Irish the imperative need to hang out in his neck of the woods on their second date. That way, her neighbor Alicia would not be able to see his large semi truck with the telling logo sticking out of her driveway at 6 A.M. Marcia was bone weary of having to recap "male sleepovers" with her neighbor.

If Marcia was able to keep her mouth shut, then she would not be subjected to DATING ADVICE. Marcia abhorred dating advice–if she was given advice on how to handle a date, she would generally do the EXACT OPPOSITE. Marcia was finally going to take charge of her personal life and leave her pals to work on their own relationships. Potentially, Marcia was soon going to be just like her pals–living in sin! Potentially, Marcia would soon be relocating to Loony Lake and would only correspond with her pals via long-distance dial-up-modem email! This thought was exciting to Marcia, especially since she had already gotten the following long-winded dating advice regarding Irish Bun:

1. Just because a man had MONEY was not a good reason to date him. This tidbit came from Alicia's mom, who was also a neighbor of Marcia's. The very same woman who advised Marcia to leave her outside condo lights on so that she and Alicia, in their side by side condos, would know when Marcia got home from a date. Marcia had told them - with a confidence she had not known she possessed–that she was NOT coming home! It was just NOT RIGHT–Marcia was 50 years old and could arrive home whenever she wanted to!

2. Money doesn't hurt. This from Alicia. Marcia was well aware that SPNW (substantial personal net worth) did not hurt, when it came to blind dates.

3. DO NOT, UNDER ANY CIRCUMSTANCES, TELL A FIRST DATE THAT THEY WILL BE MAKING AN APPEARANCE IN A BLOCKBUSTER NOVEL (AKA SCREENPLAY-IN-PROGRESS).
    Betty was only one of many female friends who thought Marcia was STARK RAVING MAD to disclose this fact. All of Marcia's friends believed this was the kind of information that would make a man run away and never be seen again. Since men were generally known for running at the slightest threat, they reasoned, why did Marcia need to push the envelope on this matter?

Marcia, to her credit, told her friends that she was only being open, honest and up-front with her date. Marcia thought her date might even feel flattered to hear he was worthy of a chapter in her novel. Marcia believed that the ultimate BOY-FOR-THE-WINTER would be able to digest information of this nature without a second thought. Marcia did not realize that, by disclosing this information so soon, she might, in fact, ruin any or all chances of getting a phone call for a second date.

Marcia's long-term goal was to acquire a pair of Irish Bun race car coveralls with her name embroidered over the left breast pocket. The coveralls would be black with red trim and embroidery. Size Medium. She would wear a black T-shirt under the coveralls and her new black and red "shape-up" tennis shoes. If Marcia could pull off custom coveralls, she might then be bold enough to ask Irish if he would consider painting her name on the side of his race car.

Of course, Marcia's friends, Betty and Mary, thought they, too, deserved to have their names painted on the side of Irish's race car. Marcia promptly nipped that idea in the bud. NO! She told them sharply, ONLY MY NAME WILL BE PAINTED ON THE FREAKING RACE CAR! Geeeeeez! Couldn't Marcia for once achieve something as unique as her name in bold letters on a race car without her friends interfering?

Betty went on to add that when Marcia got "the invite" to Loony Lake, she and Mary would be casually stopping by for a visit so that they could meet Irish. Marcia asked Betty, well, what if we're "busy?" Betty smugly told her that they would be sure to stop by during the day. Marcia did not think this would be a good idea. Betty would be sucking down Irish's Coors Lites faster than you could say "Loony Lake". Marcia would be sure NOT to disclose Irish's home address to Betty and Mary. She was in a critical phase of the Irish thang. There would be plenty of time for introductions once she had relocated to Loony Lake.

Marcia now wonders why she has gotten only one phone call FROM Irish when she had to make five phone calls TO Irish. There was something very wrong with this equation. Marcia told herself she had to stay optimistic and think positive and, above all, not be paranoid. Ultimately, all that mattered was that Irish HAD called Marcia. Marcia would just have to be patient and wait for Irish to call her again. Marcia would give Irish another chance.

Luckily, Marcia had another Whisks R Us Work Week (WWW) starting so she wouldn't have an opportunity to impulsively spill any more beans to Irish over the phone - such as the revelation that he was now a character in her blockbuster novel aka screenplay-in-progress.

"Geez", Marcia thought, "I'd better get cookies in the mail for Irish TODAY!" Baking homemade Mrs. Fields cookies for Irish would cement the second date deal, of this she was sure. Baking would also allow her to QUIT WORRYING about the damn second date. Marcia knew that men moved MUCH slower than she did. Marcia began to gather cookie baking ingredients and ignored the ringing phone...Betty, then Mary, then Betty calling again. She would wait, instead, for the "715" area code to display on her Caller ID. If Marcia could only get a second call from Irish, she was confident that she could turn him into her new BOY-FOR-THE-WINTER.

JANUARY 30–FRIDAY
DAYS TILL MUSIC CRUISE = 44
DAYS SINCE PROMISE OF CALL FROM IRISH=5
MARCIA'S BEVVIE-OF-THE-MOMENT=UFF DA SIZED PUMPKIN CHAI
BRANDI'S LYRICS (VIA HEADPHONES) THAT GET HER THRU=IN A CROWDED ROOM, I'M ALONE

Marcia was currently reviewing a FLAME.com profile with the unique handle "T-L-C-O-W-BOY". She felt compelled to perform her annual B-F-T-W (BOY-FOR-THE-WINTER) free 30-day trial on FLAME. com. It was time to pounce … more snow was forecasted. TLC's profile header had caught her eye. It read **T-L-C-O-W-BOY seeks COW-GIRL for horseback riding & roll in my 24-acre hay field. READ profile carefully.**

Facts that Marcia gleaned about TLC from his profile included:

- She would have to pass as an "actively riding" cowgirl. This would definitely be a stretch for Marcia. For some reason, the term "actively riding" made her think of a yeast infection.
- Not only did Marcia need to be a REAL cowgirl, she had to be an ATTRACTIVE cowgirl!
- Marcia would also have to learn how to "ride barrels" AND perform cowboy mounted shooting. WHAT the HELL was THAT? Marcia had never even HELD a gun, let alone shot a gun while mounted! After analyzing the photo provided, Marcia determined that people were actually getting shot at and/or potentially wounded while performing cowboy mounted shooting! Marcia, an ex-hippie at heart, yearned for local (as well as global) peace. For crying out loud!
- Marcia would be forced to watch and root for TLC's favorite football team, which was NOT the Green Bay Packers. This stumped Marcia. ALL upstanding WI residents supported the Green Bay Packers (not the freaking Detroit Lions!)

RANDOM THOUGHT: Marcia was pretty dang sure that she would be the one making home-made green chili bean dip (one of her many specialty recipes). TLC, meanwhile, would be flumped in his shiny-worn forest green corduroy Barc-A-Lounger. If this scenario became a reality, Sunday football would suck.

- Last but not least, Marcia would have to order the XP44 exercise package from STERO-MERCIAL.com. XP44 was described online as "Get perfectly ripped in 90 days! Fourteen sweat-breaking, muscle-pumping exercises designed to make over your body from WI-regular to WI-ripped in just 180 days".

  Crap, Marcia was lucky to squeeze in ten yoga balance postures and four 30-minute power walks each week. The XP44 sounded even more challenging to Marcia's flabby abs than cowboy mounted shooting!

The irony of TLC's profile was that he adamantly insisted he did NOT listen to country music. TLC loved rock and (paper, scissors) roll. Marcia was confused by this. A "roll" in the 24-acre hay field … or a waxed black Ford F150 … or, god forbid, on horseback with AC/DC pounding incessantly in the background was a disturbing visual.

On a sad note, Marcia feared that TLC was one of those cowboys who had a tightly notched cowboy belt. TLC was one of those cowboys who tried to pull a fast one on FLAME.com and encrypt his email address [whiskeystill@yahoo.com] into his profile text. Marcia, the anal editor, spotted this anomaly immediately. Profile red flag number??? By now, Marcia had lost count.

Do NOT get Marcia started on TLC's fashion sense. She knew she was hyper-critical, but PUH-LEEEEEAAASE…EEEWWWW… DISTURBING…

- For example, wasn't it illegal to turn an American flag into clothing? Marcia would have to research this. Although she was a proud U.S. citizen, a "button-down" tailored from a bright, stiff, red, white and blue flag did not appeal to her on any fashion level.
- Marcia may as well admit it…she really took issue with wranglers that rode at ribcage level on a man. She could live with an oversize rodeo-style belt buckle. But mid-waist jeans paired with an oversize western-themed belt buckle made her cringe.

- When a dual-gun leather holster was added to the above wardrobe mix, it promptly sent Marcia over the profile perusal edge. Less was more for holsters. A single-gun holster, at the most, was necessary.
- Marcia was not even gonna touch the floppy cowboy hat TLC proudly modeled. Cowboy hats were supposed to be stiff, not floppy.
- Ditto for the cowboy boots–although TLC got bonus points for the shiny brass buckles on his cowboy boots.

FEBRAURY 1–SUNDAY
DAYS TILL MUSIC CRUISE = 42
DAYS SINCE PROMISE OF CALL FROM IRISH=7
MARCIA'S BEVVIES-OF-THE-MOMENT=CHEAP MULLED WINE, LEINE'S BEER AND AN ABOVE-AVERAGE BOTTLE OF ITALIAN PINOT NOIR
BRANDI'S LYRICS (VIA HEADPHONES) THAT GET HER THRU=IN A CROWDED ROOM, I'M ALONE

A woman on FLAME.com had subscribed as a man! in order to promote her new "singles mixer" business. Marcia had now achieved the lowest of lows–getting a mass marketed email from a WOMAN on FLAME.com! Marcia was at first confused and thought the woman really WAS interested in her, even though Marcia had specifically checked the "interested in males, ages 44 - 51" box on her profile.

Once Marcia realized that the woman was emailing her to invite her to a singles mixer event in her area, Marcia had calmed down a bit. The event was to be held only five miles from Marcia's condo at an establishment called Shipwreck's, on Lower Log Lake. Shipwreck's was well known in the area because it hosted the PENGUIN PLUNGE event each winter.

This year, after the daytime Sunday Penguin Plunge event, an evening mixer would be held at Shipwreck's. The cost was twenty dollars, and it included hors d'voeures, "introduction games" and the potential to meet the man of your dreams from the "local dating pool" at FLAME. com. Marcia decided she had nothing to lose by signing up for the event, even though the thought of a woman using FLAME.com subscribers as candidates to earn income irked Marcia. There was just no free lunch in this world. Marcia thought her subscription fees alone should cover events such as this. The mixer was designed for guests to meet people that night. If anyone happened to "connect", the business throwing the gala would later send out "interest notifications." Marcia liked this low-key, non-threatening approach and decided to bury her resentment of the woman turning a profit on her and, instead, have a good attitude about the mixer.

Marcia tried to recruit Betty for the event, but Betty was busy that night. Marcia sighed at the thought of attending the mixer solo. She HATED attending solo. She NEEDED Betty's outgoing personality at an event such as this.

Marcia dressed carefully for her singles day and night on-the-town. Marcia did NOT have a curfew due to the fact that her daughter was out of the country. Marcia hoped that she would be able to take advantage of this by staying up all night talking to with a man she immediately hit it off at either the "Penguin Plunge" or the mixer.

It was hard to dress in a sexy fashion when, during the day, Marcia would be standing in eighteen degree temps. She was wearing her indigo jeans with a long-sleeved Cayamo T-shirt and her trademark hoodie, over long underwear. There was nothing worse than standing out on the lake freezing your buns off. Marcia hoped her long underwear did not make her look chunky. She would probably have to remove them that evening and change into a fresh top, as well; her current T-shirt would probably get sweat-stained. Unfortunately, her recent online clothing order that included a poppy-colored fuzzy vest had not arrived in time to wear that day.

Marcia used an extra dollop of hair elixir so that her short cut had lots of texture and depth. She added an extra splash of perfume in addition to her essential oils. She also applied a double-coat of indigo mascara, in the manner Daughter had taught her, so that her eyelashes made her brown eyes pop. She grabbed her winter coat and one of the many scarves hanging in her entryway and went to warm up the car.

The drive out to Lower Log Lake was a bit tricky. The Haystack-area back roads were not well-plowed. The parking lot at Shipwreck's was packed. Marcia smiled at the thought of a good turnout for the Penguin Plunge.

There were approximately 1,000 pickup trucks and 600 snowmobiles parked on the lake. Bleachers were set up around the spot on the lake that the ice cutters would saw an opening into, creating a rectangular hole for brave Wisconsin-ites to jump into. A hot tub was warming up so that the "plungers" could warm up their shivering bodies after they immersed themselves into the frigid water. The event would be broadcast live by a DJ from the local radio station. Food booths, which sold hot dogs, nachos with fake cheese, warm cocoa and cold beer were positioned off to one side.

Marcia located a small open spot on the bleachers to sit. She tightened her Sorrel boots and wrapped her polar fleece blanket around herself to ward off the arctic wind. She pulled her thermos of mulled wine from her backpack and poured herself a cup to sip. The bleachers were packed with people of every age–small children bundled in wool blankets, old-timers in plaid hats with flaps over their ears, inebriated young men in snowmobile suits. Coolers filled with beer took the place of picnic baskets and were used as seating.

Four men began cutting 26-inch blocks of ice from the lake. They had resorted to tedious manual work, since their power tool was not operating correctly. The men cut out each block of ice and then used a huge set of tongs to pull the ice block from the water and set it aside. After about an hour, a 6' x 4' hole had been created. It was time to begin the contest! The "plungers" lined up behind the hole. One was dressed in a Little Bo Peep outfit, complete with high heels that skittered across the ice when she walked. Another group was dressed as Tiger Woods and his caddies. The sheriff, fully uniformed, joined the line of "plungers"; his gun nestled in his holster. A few other "plungers" were dressed as giant wedges of cheese. All of the costumes were quite creative, especially for a cold February afternoon.

Once the Penguin Plunge had finished, Marcia entered the bar area where the mixer was to be held. She realized that most of the remaining cars in the parking lot represented Penguin Plunge leftovers taking advantage of the "All You Can Eat Fish Fry" in the adjacent dining room. The bar itself held a meager total of nine people - two of whom were the event's organizers. Marcia signed in to the event and received a raffle ticket for door prizes. The organizers had told Marcia that women in her age group were desperately needed at the mixer; however, Marcia did not see one man her age at the bar.

Marcia made her way to the bar where a couple (newly introduced?) sat chatting over beers. Marcia ordered a Leinie's on tap and tried to look inconspicuous. She was fashionably late; yet, she saw no one at the bar she would be interested in talking to.

A few moments later, a young, fairly handsome man sat down next to her and also ordered a Leinie's. "Geeeeez," Marcia thought, "am I going to be the token cougar at this dang event?" The young man, named Earl, was friendly enough to Marcia. He was out that night, taking a break from his live-in woman (whom he had happened to meet on a FREE DATING WEBSITE!) Earl rambled on and on about the number of "free prospects" that he had been swamped with on the free site. Marcia mentally filed the website name for possible future use.

Other people at the mixer were helping themselves to a large array of appetizers–chilled shrimp with cocktail sauce, mini wieners in BBQ sauce, crudités and veggie dip. Marcia was too self conscious to stand in line alone in order to load up a plate. She always went hungry at social gatherings such as this.

After an hour or so, approximately seventy-five people had made an appearance. The event organizers decided it was time to play "get to know you" games and instructed everyone to sit in groups of six at tables set up nearby. Marcia's table included: an older couple (who seemed to be hitting it off), two twenty-ish women in tight jeans and belly-baring tank tops, and Herbie.

Herbie was a fifty-two year old penitentiary worker. He was dressed in jeans and a plaid button-down. Herbie's glasses hailed from the 1980's and were of the oversized, tortoise shell variety. Herbie spent his weekends doing chores on the family farm, where his 86-year-old mother lived alone.

Both Herbie and Marcia won door prizes because they finished their "get to know you" games in the top five. Their door prize was a 12-pack of locally brewed beer. Marcia had by then quit drinking, but Herbie kept a "tall one" close by. He became more animated after every beer, engaging Marcia in tedious conversation. "What am I doing here?" Marcia thought. "I need to get out of here right now!" She hastily made end-of-night pleasantries to Herbie. Marcia had that "alone-in-a-crowded-room" feeling and that was her cue to leave. Marcia had a feeling that Herbie was going to express interest in dating her and she did not want to encourage him in that respect.

Marcia slowly navigated the icy roads back home. She was feeling pretty down and out. No matter what venue she tried, there were never any potential date results. She decided she would open her above-average bottle of Italian Pinot Noir when she got home and take a bubble bath. The temperature that night was forecasted to be -26 below.

Her house was warm and cozy and Marcia was glad she had made the decision to leave the mixer early. She opened the bottle of wine to air and ran the tub, using generous splashes of lavender oil and bubble bath. Once the tub was filled, she decided she would turn off the outside Christmas lights so she would not have to brave the cold after her bubble bath. Marcia went out the front door and pulled it gently closed behind her.

After Marcia had pulled out the Xmas light cord, she returned to the door and turned the doorknob. SH--! The freaking door was locked! Daughter's friends must have turned the top lock on the door without Marcia noticing. She double checked the door with the same result. Marcia was now outside in below-zero temps, dressed in her pink fleece robe patterned with martinis and her slippers! She had locked herself out of her freaking condo after only four sips of Pinot! She could, in fact, see her bottle of Pinot through her kitchen window. She had no cell phone, no coat, nothing. She tried doing deep breathing (which was hard to do in the freezing cold) and suddenly realized she could access the garage using the entry code pad. She frantically pressed the code in over and over again until the door finally creaked open. Marcia went up the steps leading to the inside door and turned the handle. That door was also locked! Marcia had, unfortunately, also locked the door after she had parked her car in the garage. There were no hidden keys to either door hidden anywhere in the garage.

Marcia peered around the cul de sac for houses with lights on. She did not want to go to her elderly neighbors—it was after eleven o'clock. She decided to try her new neighbor's house, which was still lit up. She navigated precariously over the icy road in her slippers to the new neighbor's front door. A young woman answered and Marcia introduced herself and explained her predicament. The woman, Faye, told Marcia she should try sliding a credit card along the side of the door. Faye demonstrated this on her own locked front door and it worked seamlessly! Marcia then enlisted Faye to help her attempt a credit card break-in on her front door. Faye walked with Marcia to Marcia's front porch and gave it a try, but she had no luck. Marcia's door remained locked. Marcia asked Faye if she could use Faye's cell phone to call the non-emergency police number. This turned out to be the number for the sheriff's office (the same sheriff who had taken a plunge into the icy lake earlier that day). The operator told Marcia they did not come out to try and unlock doors and that, if they did come out, they would have to smash one of Marcia's windows to get into the house. This was not an acceptable method of entry for Marcia, since a broken window in sub-zero temps would definitely cause problems. Marcia broke down and called a locksmith thirty miles away. The locksmith told Marcia he would be there in forty-five minutes. Marcia declined Faye's offer to come and stay at her house. Marcia instead opened her car trunk and found her winter survival kit items, including coat, hat, mittens and boots.

Marcia proceeded to pace through the snow drifts around her house, scoping out alternate ways to get into her house. There were no alternatives. By the time the locksmith arrived, Marcia was frozen to her core. It took the locksmith thirty-five minutes to get her front door open. Once inside, Marcia re-ran her lavender tub and polished off the entire bottle of pinot before promptly passing out, alone, in her chilly bed sheets.

FEBRUARY 7–SATURDAY
DAYS TILL MUSIC CRUISE = 36
DAYS SINCE PROMISE OF CALL FROM IRISH=13
MARCIA'S BEVVIE-OF-THE-MOMENT=TRADER JOE'S PINOT NOIR
BRANDI'S LYRICS (VIA HEADPHONES) THAT GET HER THRU=I'M HAPPY CAN'T YOU SEE, I'M ALRIGHT

The phone call came while Marcia was "holed up" in a swank hotel room at the Hole in the Hot Tub Casino (H-I-T-H-T) with her two sisters. The three of them had scheduled an emergency getaway because they were all suffering from acute cabin fever, due to the extremely harsh WI winter. Marcia and her sisters had just "hit the casino floor" to distract from the reality of the never-ending winter outside. There was nothing like being surrounded by like-minded GULLIBLE, UNSUSPECTING, CORDUROY-CLAD MIDWESTERNERS having enormous amounts of their disposable income sucked down by the extremely tight H-I-T-H-T slot machines to keep the winter blues at bay. Although in Marcia's case, it was NOT disposable income.

Marcia let the "unknown number" call go through to voice mail. She had no time for annoying phone calls. Marcia was on a mission. She had already paid her sisters 10% of her winnings–FOR A TOTAL OF $37.50 EACH–based on their long-standing "HOUSE RULE." The "House Rule" stipulated that any sister who earned $100.00 or more on a single slot machine "hit" had to pay the other sisters 10% of her winnings. Marcia was usually THE BIG A--ALL-AROUND-WINNINGEST SISTER (LUCKY, LUCKY, LUCKY). Marcia was certainly not going to interrupt her amazing 10% rule winning streak to take a (potentially boring telemarketer) phone call.

Unfortunately, the 10% rule winning streak did not last all night. The sisters, worn down by too much wine and not enough Trader Joe snacks, made the decision to retire for the night. Once they were safely snuggled in their hotel room, Marcia realized she had forgotten to check her voice mail. The phone message did NOT reveal great news. The Penguin Plunge event organizer had called to let Marcia know that Herbie was interested in setting up a date with Marcia! ARRGGHHH! Marcia moaned. It was SO typical–the man Marcia was least interested in was hot for her!

Now Marcia was going to have to compose an awkward email to Herbie, in order to let him down gently. The thought of spending her weekends doing chores with Herbie on his mother's farm was very distressing. Why could Marcia never leave a singles event with a worthy dating prospect? Why was Marcia's current date theme limited to farmers living in even more desolate parts of Wisconsin? Marcia had nothing in common with these men. Why did Marcia even continue to try? Marcia's sister's tried to console her but farmer-based-thoughts kept Marcia tossing and turning all night in the lumpy hotel bed.

Marcia woke suddenly at 5:55 the next morning, startled by the sound of her own loud, obnoxious snoring. She had shared the bed with her little sister, who was still sleeping peacefully next to her. Marcia and her sister bonded through their snoring. Their other sister, however, never got a good night's sleep during H-I-T-H-T Casino getaways because of the non-stop snoring in their room.

Marcia's sister soon awoke to the sound of Marcia rustling in the bed sheets next to her. Her sister immediately relayed the funny story of how Marcia had talked in her sleep during the night. Marcia's sister had been unable to sleep due to the volume of Marcia's snoring. She said to Marcia, "MARCIA, wake up." Marcia, still sleeping had replied, "I can't." Marcia's sister asked her "Why not?" Marcia promptly replied "I'm filing." "You're what?" asked Marcia's sister incredulously. Marcia repeated, "Filing." Marcia's sister, getting impatient by this time, asked, "What do you mean, filing?" Marcia had rolled over and mumbled "Filing, smiling, what's the difference." The two sisters now shared a laugh at the silly sleep-talking story—Marcia was always mumbling nonsensical words in her sleep. She was one of a kind. For this reason, and for the 10% house rule, the sisters treasured their H-I-T-H-T outings together.

Marcia jumped out of bed and began to dress in a hurry. She needed to get her butt down to the awards counter, toot-sweet. Marcia was on a mission to score a free mp3 player that the H-I-T-H-T was offering that morning.

The awards counter opened at 7:00 but Marcia wanted to allow extra time so that she could be one of the first people in line. Marcia's biggest pet peeve at the H-I-T-H-T Casino was the long waiting lines she had to endure just to procure one of their never-ending promotional items.

These "promos" were especially prominent during the holiday season, and included items such as: a frozen turkey; collectible boxing cards; a set of four etched fruit lemonade glasses; a frozen ham (complete with pineapple and maraschino cherries); and an Xmas wreath, which Marcia knew first-hand was wrapped in a dry cleaning bag to protect it on the trip home. Last but not least, the H-I-T-H-T offered a $3.75 holiday bonus, payable in actual cash! Free cash was a foreign concept at the casino. Regardless of the promotion, one could guarantee that 60% or more of all Wisconsin residents were liable to show up and stand in the four-hour-long line to get it. This being the recession and all.

Marcia was, however, smart enough to see these promotions as what they really were—promotions whose hidden ulterior motive could be summed up as "suck-you-in, suck-you-dry." Marcia was nothing if not realistic.

However, the "mp3 player" promo had caught her eye because she knew she would be staying at the H-I-T-H-T on the morning the promotion started. So why not take advantage of it? An mp3 player was something she would actually use, for a change.

Surprisingly, at 6:45 A.M., she was the ONLY person in line. The crowd control dividers had already been set up. Marcia snickered at the sight of the dividers—she secretly referred to them as "cattle fences." She breezed through the non-line and approached the friendly, accommodating counter person. Marcia smiled and pointed to a blue mp3 player (she had her choice of blue, red, black and silver). She could tell by the box and the weight of the mp3 player itself that it was not on the same level with an iPod Nano. Or an iPod Shuffle. Not even a Radio Shack Eclipse.

When Marcia returned to the hotel room, she showed her bonus mp3 to her sisters, who just sighed. Marcia was always the luckiest one; not only did she win the 10% rule on every freaking getaway; she also managed to snag bonus prizes as well. Marcia's sisters did, however, forgive Marcia because she had shared her previous night's winnings with them.

The sisters packed up their hotel room and went their separate ways—her sisters, to the big city of Minneapolis and Marcia to the small town of Haystack. Marcia, navigating WI back roads as usual, kept her cruise control set at a moderate 58 MPH. A few miles outside of Grazel Grove, a sheriff's car passed her. Marcia performed her usual rearview mirror "cop check." To her horror, the sheriff had pulled a U-turn and was now directly behind Marcia, lights flashing. "SH--!" Marcia thought, "all of my H-I-T-H-T Casino winnings are about to be forfeited to the state of WI for a freaking speeding ticket!"

Shaking with fright, Marcia attempted to pull over to the side of the narrow road. She began to sweat profusely. Marcia was extremely proud of her driving record–she had NEVER gotten a ticket for any kind of moving violation. The sheriff approached her window and asked Marcia for her license and insurance paperwork. This, at least, Marcia was able to promptly provide the sheriff. She mentally noted that the sheriff appeared to have a somewhat grumpy demeanor. Marcia did not want to have her fun "sister's night out" memories spoiled by the g-d sheriff. She breathed deeply.

As if turned out, Marcia's Hybrid license plates were currently registered to an Escalade in Edenborough, WI. The DMV license bureau in Haystack had, unfortunately for Marcia, transposed two letters on her license plate so that they duplicated the Escalade's. The grumpy sheriff seemed somewhat suspicious…as if Marcia were a big-time drug dealer from the WI 'burbs who had stolen the plates to cover up her hideous crack cocaine crimes. Or that Marcia somehow posed a national threat to security. Especially alarming to Marcia was the fact that she currently had two buds of "pizza" tucked away in her silver "illegal substance" case, which she had carelessly stashed in her pillowcase and thrown into the Hybrid's trunk. Marcia did not want to give the sheriff any reason to search the trunk. Marcia carefully composed her face into a friendly, cooperative expression for the sheriff, even though inside she was seething.

The sheriff asked Marcia if she had ever been pulled over before for this license plate violation. "What a dork," Marcia thought, "Does this guy really think I would be stupid enough to leave such a blatant DMV user-error uncorrected?" Marcia was paranoid enough about transporting minute amounts of pizza as it was. Marcia smiled brightly and was able to charm the grumpy sheriff out of a ticket by pointing out her spotless driving record and assuring him that she would rectify the illegal license plate issue that very day. Marcia's would now have to turn over her entire

H-I-T-H-T winnings to the state of WI to fix some incompetent DMV worker's mistake.

Once the sheriff was on his way, Marcia sat, hands on steering wheel, composing herself. Whew, she thought, that could have been bad. Marcia had narrowly escaped being hauled in for illegal substances. She would be more than happy to sacrifice her H-I-T-H-T winnings for a new license plate.

FEBRARY 11–WEDNESDAY
DAYS TILL MUSIC CRUISE = 32
DAYS SINCE PROMISE OF CALL FROM IRISH=17
MARCIA'S BEVVIE-OF-THE-MOMENT=THE NASTY BOTTLE OF GNARLY HEAD 2005 MERLOT (CA) IN HER SPECIAL SIMILAR-TO-CRUISE-TYPE-WINE GLASS
BRANDI'S LYRICS (VIA HEADPHONES) THAT GET HER THRU=YOU CAN'T BREAK A HEART THAT WASN'T EVEN YOURS TO BREAK

The Whisks R Us Work Week (WWW) dragged by slowly after the sisters H-I-T-H-T getaway. Marcia, despite being the big winner, was extremely broke. On a whim, she decided to try the new FREE dating website that Earl from the singles mixers had recommended. Marcia was well aware of the fact that subscribers sometimes got what they paid for on free dating sites but she felt she had nothing to lose at this point. She had heard good things about the site and hoped maybe she could just meet a guy to hang out with in Hayward, nothing serious. The site would be thoughtful enough to send Marcia daily potential "matches." Marcia was always appreciative of others doing her work for her. She was also excited about the "little extras" the free site provided, such as flowers, candy, and stuffed animals that could be used to express interest in other members.

After a few weeks of browsing and sending out "feelers" (with no response, as usual), Marcia came across a photo of a man sitting casually on the front steps of a nice looking brick and stucco home. A large log lay nearby the man; Marcia immediately saw the potential for romantic evenings spent by the fireplace, which always got her imagination going, especially on a cold WI winter day. Marcia decided to write the man a short, witty note (her usual modus operandi). There was an immediate reply from the man, equally witty! Marcia fired off a note back to him and soon they were emailing back and forth. His name was Curtis. He seemed like a perky, happy guy. Because Curtis was from Minneapolis, they arranged to have a drink at a restaurant off Highway 65 when Marcia was working in the big city at the Whisks R Us Warehouse later that week.

The plan was soon modified, however, when Marcia called Curtis the next day on her way to Hayward from the eastern metro. Curtis suggested she meet him right then and there, a few days before their scheduled date. Marcia was a bit nervous–her Jones New York cotton dress was a little road-weary and her hair did not look as bouncing and behaving as it had that morning. But still—she did look pretty damn cute. Marcia decided—what the heck? She was excited to meet Curtis and it was always better to get the initial encounter behind her.

Marcia arrived first at the Mexican-themed bar and was told by the waiter it was Happy Hour. Marcia indulged in not one, but two, margaritas. Frozen margaritas were not on the list of Happy Hour drinks so she had to settle for margaritas on-the-rocks. After a few minutes of sitting alone, a man, wearing a striped short-sleeved sport shirt and jeans, came blasting through the front door. "OMG," Marcia thought, "this is NOT Curtis. This cannot possibly be Curtis." He was much heavier than his front-step photo and had "reader" glasses propped on his big head. He approached her with a big smile, like he was all that. Marcia knew immediately that she was not attracted to him, but decided to sip her drink and make the best of it. After all, looks were not everything and she appreciated the sense of humor that Curtis conveyed through his emails.

Curtis introduced himself, sat down and asked what Marcia was drinking. He seemed quite self-confident, a good attribute. He did not, however, have enough money to buy himself (or her) a drink. Marcia inwardly groaned. Marcia should have run for the hills as soon as this fact was revealed. But Marcia gave him the benefit of the doubt - he DID work on commission and there WAS a recession going on.

The two of them chatted for a few minutes and their date seemed to be going well. Nevertheless, Marcia knew that she should probably finish her drinks and leave as soon as was (politely) possible. Curtis seemed like a swell guy, but there were no sparks flying for Marcia. The margarita(s), however, were affecting her good judgment.

While sitting together, Marcia and Curtis were interrupted by a pretty, heavily made-up woman who knew Curtis. She was sitting nearby at the bar as part of a birthday party-in-progress. The woman asked Curtis what he was doing there, and Curtis replied that he was "on a date" with Marcia. The woman seemed surprised that Curtis was there, sitting with a cute, seemingly intelligent woman like Marcia. Marcia added this to her "red flag" list, especially after the woman left and Curtis disclosed the fact that he used to live with her. He told Marcia he had re-done her roof and she had never paid him for it. Curtis was angry with the woman, and spent the remainder of their date dissing her profusely.

As it turned out, Curtis was not the OWNER of the beautiful brick and stucco home—he was, in fact, a SQUATTER. He currently had one unemployed roommate, whose role it was to prepare amazing gourmet meals for himself and Curtis. At any given time, there could be several roommates in the 4,000 square foot home, most of them unemployed and/ or down on their luck. Curtis was the quintessential landlord, collecting rent and utility money from each of them, depending on their ability to pay. The unlawful tenants were so behind on their heat bill, they used the log from Curtis's photo (and other wood hauled in via Curtis's pickup truck) to heat the home. The electricity, too, was in constant danger of being cut off.

Marcia did not learn all of these facts until several weeks later. She was in such a fragile state of low self-esteem that these facts did not really register. Marcia had always been good at chipping in on dates, but this date took the cake. Curtis's idea of a date was to rent movies (or, even better, tap into the free cable TV that his cable-guy buddy had hooked up for an even more cost-effective way of watching movies). Of course, Marcia and Curtis were never alone at the house…there was always an assortment of buddies hanging out on any given night. Their idea of entertainment seemed to be "manly" things like roasting a large portion of pig in a special roaster or BBQ-ing on the deck with the nice view. Most of Curtis's buddies drank like fish. The backyard deer were fed with corn Curtis and his roommate purchased, even if this meant no toilet paper for the household.

Everyone seemed surprised that Curtis was "dating", which to Marcia was OK; she was still, after zillions of red flags, giving him the benefit of the doubt. He DID have a great sense of humor, even though he was SO NOT her type. Marcia was good about helping out with movie or gas money for Curtis. Soon, however, the ultimate red flag was raised - Curtis asked to borrow $40.00 from Marcia. "OMG," Marcia thought, "here we go." Marcia and Curtis had been joking about Marcia being the "sugar mama" for a few weeks by this time but Marcia was naive enough not to believe this could really be happening. Curtis had, to his credit, promptly paid Marcia back the $40.00, which put Marcia's mind at ease a bit.

One night, on a payday, (Curtis had actually gotten paid a commission!) Curtis told Marcia to dress up and "come on down" as he was going to take her out for sushi. There was an excellent sushi restaurant nearby, he said, and they would go on an actual date together. Marcia fretted for a few hours about what she would wear but finally decided on her brown CK cords with a cute fleece-lined hoodie and scarf tied decoratively around her neck. She did not wear her crocs - Curtis hated crocs. Marcia was excited to finally go out in public with Curtis. Once Marcia arrived at Curtis's, however, she immediately knew it would not be sushi night out after all. Curtis's phone had gotten cut off that morning for non-payment of his bill. He was in a terrible mood. His roommate tried to compensate by whipping up loaded stuffed baked potatoes with grilled steak and salad. Curtis, usually the first one at the household buffet line, sat morosely on the sagging couch, drinking beer and chain-smoking.

The house that Curtis "occupied" was at one time a mansion but now the forest green carpet in the living room and the dark wood in the kitchen were outdated. There was not enough furniture in the house to fill up the 4,000 square feet. A 4-foot big screen TV dominated the family room, where the fireplace was located (in other rooms of the house, you could almost see your breath). Someone had to constantly feed the fire, especially at night, in order to keep the pipes from freezing.

The family room was THE spot for endless male "Poker Nights." Curtis somehow managed to procure serving tables and silver plated serving dishes for the full-course Asian meals his roommate would prepare, which included homemade spring rolls, chicken fried rice and moo shoo pork. Curtis invited Marcia to come over on poker nights and serve drinks in a sexy maid outfit, but Marcia declined. She wondered if Curtis had any single friends who had it together better than he did. Curtis started his independent work days around 10:00 AM and usually finished them by 3:00. This schedule did not mesh well with diligent Marcia, the hard-working whisk rep. Curtis had his own large office in the home, strewn with "lead" sheets and miscellaneous debris.

Curtis's bedroom also included a big screen TV - this one was only 3 feet wide. Marcia was beginning to wonder if all Curtis did was lie in bed and watch TV all day. The master bathroom was a sight to behold—it was done up in maroon and silver orchid wallpaper, with a large Jacuzzi tub, shower, multiple sinks and a toilet. The fixtures were gold plated. There was such a contrast between the gold-plated bathroom fixtures and the lack of heat in the home. Curtis and his roommate were currently awaiting an eviction notice and/or the sheriff to show up knocking at their front door.

Marcia began to sense that Curtis was a classic sales personality, known to scam his way through life versus forking over cold hard cash. On his FREE dating website profile, he came across as a successful, hard-working guy. In reality, he was looking for a SUGAR MAMA. Marcia could not afford to be a SUGAR MAMA. She sensed that Curtis was a "scammer" because there was always some new electronic equipment appearing at Curtis's house, something he had traded one or another of his meager possessions for. Curtis's priorities included: how to get money to buy groceries, how to get money to buy beer, how to keep the creditors off his back, and how to collect rent from his merry-go-round flock of roommates. This was not something Marcia needed to be a part of and she knew it, knew it at her very first meeting with Curtis when he could not even buy his own drink. Marcia knew she had better collect her chicken fried rice casserole currently sitting in Curtis's cupboard and get the hell out before she got in any deeper.

Marcia now turned her attention back to Curtis, whining on his saggy couch. If only his phone bill could get settled up, he lamented. How could he possibly do business without cellular service? Times were tough, sales-wise, and he had gotten a little (a little!) behind on the bills. The gas company wanted a $540 payment by next Tuesday. The electricity company was also hounding him and could cut off his 4- foot TV at any time, in the height of football season. He knew spring would bring bigger, better sales if he could only make it till then. Of course Marcia felt horrible about Curtis's situation. Of course Marcia told Curtis she could write the cell phone company a check so that he could get service restored. Marcia KNEW Curtis would be good for the money–hadn't he repaid her the cash he had earlier borrowed?

The next day, Marcia the nice, sweet, vulnerable gal accompanied Curtis to the cell phone store near his "mansion" and applied $140 of her personal funds toward his account so that his cell phone would get turned back on. Curtis earnestly promised to repay Marcia ASAP and Marcia took him at his word.

Weeks later, when Marcia had stopped going to Curtis's for movie aka "roommate" dates, Marcia emailed Curtis about the money owed to her. Curtis's response to Marcia was, in these exact words, "BITE ME." "Are you kidding me?" Marcia thought, "BITE ME?" She had paid Curtis's phone bill, for cripes sake! Wasn't there a shred of morality left in men anymore? Marcia was shocked at the audacity of this man. Marcia realized then that Curtis was an evil man. The woman at the restaurant did not owe HIM money for re-doing her roof; HE probably owed the woman rent money instead. Marcia had finally come to her senses, asking herself, what the hell she had done, getting involved with Curtis. She was old enough to know better. Was she so desperate for companionship that she had stooped to this new dating low? Why was she such a loser magnet? When would she ever learn to trust her initial gut feeling and run for the freaking hills? Marcia decided that being out $140 was worth learning a valuable lesson from Curtis. Marcia was extremely tired of being taken advantage of. Marcia needed to find the guy who would treat her like a queen!

Marcia now needed to regroup and get the heck off of the free dating site. Of course Curtis would be on a FREE site; the guy was a squatter, for cripes sake. Marcia was NOT a loser, nor was Marcia a SUGAR MAMA! Marcia was only too freaking nice and gullible. Even though Marcia was traumatized, she needed to forget about Curtis and move on with her life. Curtis would never be worthy of being her BOY-FOR-THE-WINTER. In Marcia's eyes, Curtis was not even worthy of BOY-FOR-THE-NIGHT.

FEBRUARY 17–TUESDAY
DAYS TILL MUSIC CRUISE=26
DAYS SINCE PROMISE OF CALL FROM IRISH=23
MARCIA'S BEVVIE-OF-THE-MOMENT=STRONG FRENCH ROAST WITH 1/2 & 1/2 AND A HEALTHY DOLLUP OF KAHLUA
BRANDI'S LYRICS (VIA HEADPHONES) THAT GET HER THRU=IN A CROWDED ROOM, I'M ALONE

As if her "Free website" date was not enough to drive Marcia crazy, the president of the "DOLL HOUSE" condo association, Bertha-Birdbrain-Be-otch (Marcia's codename for the nosy, in-her-face president), informed her grandkids that Marcia had a hole in her hot tub. One of the grandkids promptly relayed this info to Marcia's daughter via FACESPACE.COM. Marcia's daughter, in turn, relayed this info to Marcia via email from Germany. Marcia went out to inspect the hot tub. Marcia saw no ice build-up underneath the hot tub, although, it being winter, a leak was going to be hard to diagnose. Marcia concluded that there were no leaks in her hot tub. However, since the snow drifts in her backyard averaged 4 feet that winter, Marcia was unable to see that some punk had thrown a rock the size of east Texas at the far side of the hot tub, puncturing the outer plastic shell. She now realized, in horror that the entire side of her hot tub was cracked and was rapidly falling into her backyard in jagged pieces.

Marcia quickly switched into her least favorite role, that of "home maintenance handy-woman." She located her most trusted home repair tool–the roll of duct tape. Marcia efficiently triple-duct-taped together what remained of her hot tub shell in order to salvage it enough to get through the rest of the Wisconsin winter. While viciously ripping off 3 foot pieces of duct tape, she muttered her usual home repair mantra–"I am NOT a freaking' handywoman. I cannot possibly maintain all this stuff by myself." These words miraculously helped her to complete the chilly, painful hot tub repair process.

Back inside her condo sipping coffee with Kahlua (to warm herself, she justified), Marcia recalled happier hot tub times. She distinctly remembered the last gorgeous Indian summer day she had actually USED her hot tub. She had blended up a strong margarita to sip while soaking in the hot tub, knowing it was one of the last opportunities for "snow-free hot tubbing." Marcia now conveniently forgot about the black and yellow wasps that had oozed continuously from below her back door while hot-tubbing that afternoon. She conveniently forgot about having to empty her entire "20% value sized" bottle of hornet spray under the back step, while crouching soaking wet in her bathing suit. Instead, she focused on the memory of the yellow, red, brown and blue mini M & M packages that had floated around her patio on that sunny afternoon. Marcia had equated the M & M package colors to some of her favorite songs–"Yellow" and "Blue." That day, Marcia had felt multi-dimensional because of all the colors that had surrounded her.

Now Marcia tried to rouse herself from the pleasant, colorful memories of that autumn afternoon. It seemed so long ago. She must quit daydreaming and subject herself to yet another unpleasant homeowner chore–opening the mail. Marcia propped up her feet, which were ironically covered with yellow bruises from acupuncture for pain management. The stack of bills was staggering–Marcia did not know where to begin. It might be best if she simply stayed in the warmth of her color-infused memories and, instead, pinched a hit of pot from her emergency stash stored in her great-uncle Hank's yellow "TOP" cigarette tobacco tin. Marcia generally used her emergency stash only in case of extreme "pain management" but today she felt that tackling the enormous stack of bills fell neatly into that category. Today, it might be best if Marcia just skipped opening her stack of bills altogether.

Marcia relocated herself to her great-uncle Hank's vintage floral "smoking chair", which she had won in a family furniture lottery. The chair had been positioned in the sunniest corner of her living room. Marcia had accented "Hank's memorial corner" with his stand-up ashtray (another lottery score) and his yellow "TOP" cigarette tobacco tin. Marcia recklessly decided to spend the remainder of the afternoon entertaining herself by: a) opening a bill; b) taking a "TOP" one-hit to offset the bill's shock value, and c) using her one-hit lighter to start each bill on fire. This strategy, although completely out of character, proved to be an extremely effective way to erase all traumatic "bill memories" from Marcia's head. Once Marcia had reduced her bills to a harmless pile of ashes, she found a much more meaningful project to occupy her time–painting another one of great-uncle Hank's medicine chests in bright, vivid watercolors. She was pretty sure great-uncle Hank would approve.

FEBRUARY 22–SUNDAY
DAYS TILL MUSIC CRUISE = 21
DAYS SINCE PROMISE OF CALL FROM IRISH=28
MARCIA'S BEVVIE-OF-THE-MOMENT = URBANISTA COLUMBIAN, NICARAGUAN AND SUMATRAN BLEND CUSTOM ROASTED COFFEE WITH LAND O' LAKES MINI-MOO'S 1/2 AND 1/2
BRANDI'S LYRICS (VIA HEADPHONES) THAT GET HER THRU=YOU CAN'T BREAK A HEART THAT WASN'T EVEN YOURS TO BREAK

Marcia's B-F-T-W (BOY-FOR-THE-WINTER) free 30-day trial on FLAME.com was quickly coming to an end. Marcia had, by now, been sucked in to the FLAME.com review rhythm. It was Sunday morning, after all, and that was the OPTIMAL time of the week to review profiles. Even though deer hunting ended that day in WI, most of the FLAME.com men would never dream of leaving their "camo-covered" laptops behind when traveling up north. A large percentage, in fact, even brought their laptops with them to their freaking deer stands. The pre-dawn Wisconsin woods were filled with scattered fantasy "love lights" glowing from 25-foot high, hastily constructed platforms. Marcia breathed a silent prayer that some of these WI hunters still believed in true love.

Marcia clicked on the *NEWEST & HOTTEST PROFILES* tab at FLAME.com. The B-F-T-W pressure was on. Mixed precip was currently falling outdoors and measurable snow was forecasted for later that day. This meant that Marcia was only able to smoke half of a cig at a time (versus six cigs) for fear of slipping and cracking her head open while she lollygagged outside on the slick concrete.

The FLAME.com results tab displayed not one but TWO new profiles. The first, using the handle "HorseWhiskerer", did not appeal to Marcia. She sighed and clicked on the second profile. It was her last chance of the day. When she saw the profile header, Marcia did a double take…she could not believe what she was reading.

The profile header screamed in big BOLD lettering: **"HORSE PLUNDERER: SAVE A HORSE…I HOPE YOU KNOW THE REST."**

The HORSE PLUNDERER profile read as such:

Save a Horse… (You Know the Rest) is one of my favorite pastimes. I am a successful, professional dude ranch owner/cowboy poet/"Cook-Out King"/ amateur golf pro. I perform guitar gigs at campfires for my dudes and dude-ette clients. I own a "summer" ranch in Wisconsin and a "winter" ranch in Arizona. I have eighteen JACK DANIELS-BRED horses and offer trail rides at my ranch. I also raise cattle and lasso wild turkeys for sport.

I have been searching all my dude-years for a "Cook-Out Queen" to join me at the campfire court. Cabin cleaning experience is a plus. I won't guarantee I will always treat my special gal like a queen, but I can offer her a stable ranch life. My "Cook-Out Queen" preferably wears jeans that fit her like a glove. She must be a passionate kisser and must like "Saving a Horse…" on a regular basis.

"Cook-Out Queen" prospects should also be open to travel in the Black Hills for cowboy poet performances. Harmonica and/or tambourine experience is also a plus. Come explore the "wild side" of the "Cook-Out King!"

Marcia was extremely skeptical about this profile, especially after honing in on "cabin cleaning experience." To even consider making contact with Horse Plunderer would be an extreme stretch. But Marcia's free 30-day trial would be ending in only a few days! She had to take advantage of receiving premium FLAME.com services at no charge. Marcia decided to take one last "plunge" at FLAME.com. She impulsively fired off a brief, witty, intro message to Horse Plunderer.

A response from Horse Plunderer was immediate. Marcia, after carefully reading the reply, spotted an enormous red flag. HORSE PLUNDERER aka "Cook-Out King" aka "Rusty" had obviously been though the "on-line dating ropes" before. His email informed Marcia that, if she would provide her REAL email address, he would forward his custom "date kit" to her. What the hell is a "date kit", Marcia mused. Is this some kind of online scam?

Marcia went out to the patio to ponder the "Plunderer." She had added a dollop of Bailey's to her morning French Roast for insight. What do I have to lose, thought Marcia, after a hefty swig of coffee. Rusty had not, after all, asked for her credit card number. She could always resort to "Sorry, I'm leaving on a cruise" as an excuse if things got ugly with Rusty.

The next day, Marcia received, via Fed X, her "date kit" from Rusty. Included in the kit were the following items:

- A HOMEMADE, INSTRUCTIONAL AUDIO (EIGHT-TRACK) TAPE TO LISTEN TO BEFORE A DATE WAS ARRANGED
  Marcia wasn't sure how she was going to pull this off. She had invested in a $10,000 Bose sound system the previous week that did NOT include an eight-track player. She could check in her garage—there were many electronic relics stored out there. Marcia kept meaning to take her outdated equipment to the Haystack Pawn Shop to offset the payment on the Bose system. It might turn out to be a lucky omen that she had not.

- A BROCHURE OUTLINING RUSTY'S DATING "PLAN."
  The dating brochure was printed on the finest quality "green" paper and the photos were breathtaking. Well, for the most part. Rusty's latest photo looked NOTHING like his FLAME.com profile photo. In the brochure photo, Rusty was sporting a thin, blonde, scary, 10-inch waxed moustache. Five inches on either side. Freaky AND disturbing to Marcia. The moustache did NOT accentuate Rusty's thin, lined face. Instead, it accentuated his leathered jowls. Rusty did not have a thick and bushy moustache like other men Marcia had encountered during her "Western phase." Rusty had a one-of-a-kind authentic Arizona moustache… right here in northern Wisconsin! Rusty might THINK he was going to have a large percentage of WI Wrangler-wearing women smitten from the get-go. Marcia, however, would NOT be one of them. Marcia would need to have "THE MOUSTACHE TALK" with Rusty before things got serious.

- A BACKGROUND CHECK AND DISCLAIMER FORM. As noted, Rusty would order a background check if he felt one was necessary before a date. Marcia hoped this did not mean she had to go back to the HOSPITAL for STD screenings. Although Marcia certainly had nothing to hide—she had not been involved in any romantic interludes for months.

- A HOMEMADE GOLF "SCORECARD" TO RECORD POTENTIAL BONUS DATING POINTS. The sloppily-designed scorecard was broken down into categories that included "Number of Strokes", "Birdies", "Bogeys" and "Double Bogeys." Although Marcia could kick butt with a wooden driver, she was NOT sure what to think of a man who billed himself as a "wanna-be" golf pro. And Marcia could only IMAGINE, in Rusty's convoluted way of thinking, what "number of strokes" might refer to. Marcia also had grave concerns about how Rusty might use "Birdies", "Bogeys" and "Double Bogeys" (she had no clue what these terms meant in REAL golfing terms). Rusty had also included a "Ladies Handicap", which Marcia felt would surely not be necessary in her case. As for the "Par" category…hmmmm… Marcia quickly determined "Cook-Out Queens" that fell into this category would not last long on Rusty's special scorecard.

Rusty seemed, in some respects, to be a damn good catch. But there were other red flags. For example, Rusty indicated that he was a 54-year-old man seeking women ages 25-52. He claimed to be "ATHLETIC AND TONED." Marcia went back to study his brochure photos more closely. How, exactly, did Rusty's flannel-clad beer belly, which was the size of Pittsburg, translate to "athletic and toned?" Rusty must have been talking about OTHER body parts that he had maintained. Marcia could clearly see that Rusty had lean buns from riding his horse, "Whiskey", for hours each day (daily riding was paramount for all lonely cowboys). In fact, Rusty's buns appeared to be even a bit on the bony side, which was not a big turn on for Marcia. Marcia liked buns that had some meat on them. Mutual butt massages were one of Marcia's favorite bedtime activities after a long hard day.

Marcia also needed to consider how much she would have to invest, wardrobe-wise, for a potential date with Rusty. She would probably have to buy an actual pair of stretch Wranglers just for the occasion. And a flannel shirt that actually conformed to her curves (NOT her usual size XXL). And a pink bandana. And a white leather vest (vests were NOT typically very flattering on Marcia's curvy figure). And cowgirl boots with pink swirls to offset the shiny new brown leather. And an aqua straw cowgirl hat, embellished with coral stones. The list went on and on. Marcia already knew these items would not end up in the "most-worn" section of her closet. Marcia was, after all, so broke she was utilizing a freaking FREE online dating trial! She would have to carefully consider the investment versus the payoff of a "Rusty cowboy poet date."

Marcia went on to imagine what a "Rusty cowboy poet date" would actually consist of. Dinner would be served at Rusty's campfire ring on a man-made WI mountain. It would be simple–probably Dinty Moore Beef Stew with a crusty loaf of sourdough and cheap white wine, served in thermos cups. Make that Coors Lite out of the can. The alternate dinner menu option would be roasted weenies on sticks, in order to test and celebrate their shared cookout skills. Rusty would even have packed s'more ingredients, thinking he was "going all out." Marcia groaned at the thought of this. Did she not deserve an actual restaurant surf 'n turf dinner in return for her $555 clothing investment? The "highlight" of the evening (according to Rusty) would probably be Rusty the "cowboy poet" himself, strumming his sub-par guitar and crooning western love songs to Marcia. Marcia would have to endure said songs, regardless of whether she liked the corny lyrics or not.

Rusty had casually mentioned in his email that he was looking for a female companion to escort him to the New Year's Eve Rooster Ranch Rodeo. Rusty was billed at the rodeo as one of the star acts. If Rusty and Marcia clicked, Marcia could cheer Rusty on from the bleachers as a way to further "bond." Marcia could only imagine how much FREAKING CASH this event would cost her. She knew it was always best to be on top of her fashion game when dealing with rodeo dances, and cowboys-at-large. Black pleather stilettos instead of ballet flats, fishnet stockings instead of semi-hairy legs, spanx for an hourglass figure (mandatory at rodeo dances), an actual bra, a sexy black lace-trimmed bra, for cripes sake (or did cowboys prefer red lace? Marcia never had figured this out) and new mascara to replace her current dried-out tube. Freaking new hot pink lipstick, something Marcia frowned upon. All of these little extras added up, dollar-wise.

RANDOM THOUGHT: Marcia may need to re-think the fishnet stocking idea and purchase black, opaque stockings instead. Marcia had, the previous week, badly injured her thigh while dancing to her favorite song on the radio. Marcia had gotten a little wild with her dance moves, and, as a result, was severely suffering for it. She currently sported a bruise the size of a grapefruit on her left thigh. Marcia did not think this would make such a good impression on Rusty. What possible explanation would there be for an injury of this kind? Rough-housing with another cowboy? "Grapefruit hip" as Marcia lovingly referred to it, would need to stay safely tucked away for the night under her rodeo dress.

The dress for the rodeo dance would have to be frilly, flirty and fuchsia with black net accents. Cut low enough to enhance Marcia's just-right cleavage without making her boobs spill out of the sides. Her bare upper arms were enough of a problem without boob spillage. Marcia had ordered some arm "wing flab" reduction cream the week before and it already seemed to be helping. She could have her black embroidered shawl from Barcelona handy, in case of an arm flab emergency. Marcia knew that a fuchsia dress, accented with a big black satin bow at the base of her spine, would be a knock-out. Simply stunning! Marcia knew that Rusty's bloodshot eyes would pop out of his head! Marcia knew that Rusty would probably not be riding his favorite horse, "Whiskey", in the rodeo that night, or any night that month IF she played her cards right. Marcia knew that the rodeo dress would be enough to entice bony-butt Rusty. Marcia now needed to figure out if Rusty was worth enticing. Marcia was "game on" for romance and a Long-Term-Relationship. But the question remained - was Rusty BOY-FOR-THE-WINTER material?

Other potential dating scenarios might include Marcia and Rusty "hooking up" in Whiskey's stable stall, fragrant with the smell of hay and fresh horse bunud. AKA horse sh--. A corner of the stable would be cleared so that there would be room for a candlelit table, set for two. Marcia cringed at the thought of this. Even a horse TRAILER date with Rusty, which might lend itself to more ambiance and privacy (based on Rusty's brochure, he had himself one fancy horse trailer) would be claustrophobic and not conducive, in Marcia's eyes, to quality romance.

The only saving locale Rusty had to offer was his freaking RANCH IN THE DESERT! From the brochure description, the ranch sat high above the fault line on a mountain ridge, with an amazing view of the stars and Rusty's surrounding acreage. The ranch could potentially be Marcia's goal for NEXT Xmas! It was currently February. Marcia was going to have to work quickly to pull off the desert ranch for the following Xmas. Marcia could even recycle the Farmer Tony farm Xmas ornament her mom had given her for good luck. The ornament had potential to get her to the freaking ranch in the desert THAT MUCH SOONER (and hopefully, allow her to bypass any stall or trailer dates with Rusty). Marcia made a mental note to add the farm ornament to her Charlie Brown Xmas tree (which, coincidentally, stayed up year-round at Marcia's house). The farm ornament would balance out the lone red ornament on the Xmas tree perfectly. Marcia would touch the miniature farm each morning at 4:44 A.M. for good luck and then press her thumbs together for bonus German good luck.

Marcia decided that she would hold off on the MUSTACHE TALK with Rusty until after she had secured her ticket to the New Year's Eve Rooster Ranch Rodeo. Only because tickets to this event were extremely difficult to get - she didn't want to jeopardize her chances of attending. Come 2012, however, they would need to schedule a mustache "sit down." It was all part of the "give and take" of a relationship.

Suddenly, Marcia was jolted out of her daydreaming by the sound of new mail arriving in her "Inbox." Mail from Rusty! "OMG!" All Marcia had to do was THINK UP possible scenarios and the cowboy poet was all over her! She quickly clicked on her "New Mail" button to open the email. Sadly, Rusty was NOT writing to say that Marcia had made such a great first impression online that she could skip his "date kit" application. Rusty was NOT writing to say he already missed Marcia's bubbly personality that had flowed like honey (via email) to his starving heart. Rusty WAS writing to curtly inform Marcia that he had, just that morning, found his GIRL-FOR-THE-WINTER in the form of Louise, a busty, big-red-haired cowgirl from Oklahoma. Rusty was not even kind enough to apologize in the email. "ARE YOU KIDDING ME?" Marcia thought. She had just spent three quarters of her Sunday fantasizing about Rusty! In her mind, the fuchsia dress and matching accessories were already hanging in her closet! Instead, Marcia was no longer even UNDER CONSIDERATION for the New Year's Eve Rooster Ranch Rodeo with Rusty. In fact, it would behoove her to forget about Rusty as soon as possible, in terms of a BOY-

FOR-THE-WINTER. Marcia choked back tears of disappointment and promptly reached for her cell phone. Margaritas with Betty were definitely in order. Betty was ALWAYS willing to listen to another one of Marcia's potential DISASTER DATES. It was obvious that Marcia had gotten quite "rusty" at online dating. Betty would help Marcia to purge Rusty the cowboy poet from her head ASAP.

FEBRUARY 28–SATURDAY
DAYS TILL MUSIC CRUISE=15
DAYS SINCE PROMISE OF CALL FROM IRISH=34
MARCIA'S BEVVIE-OF-THE-MOMENT = STARBUCKS CAPPUCINO PRIMO MADE IN HER NEW COFFEEMAKER
BRANDI'S LYRICS (VIA HEADPHONES) THAT GET HER THRU=IN A CROWDED ROOM, I'M ALONE

Marcia, at an all-time low, had contacted the support group known as "Misfits without Money" (MWM). She dialed the MWM number and was connected after waiting several minutes (thus incurring long distance charges she could ill-afford). The prestigious President of MWM, Mort, was on another call when Marcia finally got through to the receptionist, so Marcia left her name and phone number. This would prove to be a big mistake.

Later that day, Marcia got a call back from Mort the MWM "Prez." Marcia and Mort spoke by phone for more than thirty minutes. Mostly job talk, interspersed with random "single misfit" talk. Marcia got a rundown of all scheduled MWM activities in the upcoming month. Mort also casually mentioned that a retirement party for a MWM member was being held that very night at "Stories" in nearby Storm Cave. Marcia was welcome to stop by, if she wanted to.

At that point in their phone conversation, Mort had TOTALLY switched gears and asked Marcia if she would like to place an order for steak knives! Mort, oblivious to Marcia's shock and dismay upon hearing his "pitch", went on to describe the different knife sizes, the different blade types and the lifetime warranty, all in excruciating detail. "OMG, ENOUGH ALREADY," Marcia thought, as Mort droned on and on, "I AM CURRENTLY CHARGING MY RENT. WHAT THE HELL IS THIS GUY EVEN TALKING ABOUT? WHAT HAVE I GOTTEN MYSELF INTO?"

Marcia was NOT a good steak-knife prospect. Marcia was NOT even a good "purchase-Cheddar-Goldfish-crackers-for-Daughter-at-grocery-store" prospect. Marcia had NO CASH. The fleeting thought occurred to Marcia that she might, indeed, purchase the damn steak knives and use them to cut the phone line connecting her and Mort. On second thought, she remembered her current "misfit" status and thought better of it. She had to quit being so freaking judgmental. Steak knives aside, Mort sounded like a very nice guy. Marcia needed to give MWM, and Mort, a CHANCE.

After much persuasion, Betty agreed to accompany Marcia to the MWM retirement party that night. Marcia and Betty had no idea of what to expect at a MVM function. When they arrived at Stories, they positioned themselves at the ornate bar. That way, they could secretly sneak peeks at the retirement party, currently in progress in an attached banquet room.

Betty spotted Mort right away. He was a stocky, dark-haired, 36-year-old who could easily pass for a 50 year-old, attired in an orange and teal brightly patterned silk (or was that polyester?) shirt. A thick gold chain hung around his thick neck. He had a broad, toothy smile that seemed permanently plastered on his face. His smile was NOT one of his better features.

Marcia and Betty steeled themselves and walked into the banquet room. Mort saw them enter the room and immediately approached the women. Once introductions were made, Marcia found herself assessing her feelings toward Mort–a quick "self-check" of sorts. She was not feeling any first impression spark of attraction toward Mort. Instead, Marcia felt a sharp spark of revulsion course through her. She smiled brightly and reminded herself that she needed to keep an open mind for now. "Geez, Marcia," she inwardly chastised herself, "give the poor guy a chance."

Mort, on the other hand, seemed instantly smitten by cute, bubbly Marcia. She was, after all, an infusion of fresh personality at the MWM party. After being rejected by a potential dance partner, Mort latched onto Marcia, and asked her instead to be his "first-runner-up" dance partner. Marcia awkwardly replied that the band would have to play "Brown Eyed Girl" by Van Morrison before she would feel like dancing. Marcia later thanked her lucky stars that "Brown Eyed Girl" had not played that night–she had no desire to dance with Mort.

There were several MWM members attending the celebration. The party room had a festive feel. Purple and silver balloons in recycled Martinelli bottles decorated each of the banquet tables. Once Marcia and Betty realized that many of the MWM members did not drink alcohol, they had the bartender discreetly hide their (previously purchased) bottle of Korbel. The bartender swiftly tucked the bottle into an ice bucket under the bar and gave them a conspiratorial wink.

Even boosted by their taboo champagne, Marcia and Betty felt a bit intimidated about actually joining the MWM group. Some members were laughing and chatting with one another; others were standing uneasily by themselves in the party room. Marcia and Betty made a gracious attempt to talk with Mort and some of the other members for an hour or so. The conversation was stilted. Based on Marcia's covert observations, she got the distinct impression that Mort seemed to think he was "all that." Mort was not "all that." Mort was "none of that"–none of what Marcia was looking for in a man, anyway.

Mort obviously knew EVERYONE in the room and made sure Marcia took notice of this. As the night progressed and more Martenelli was consumed, Mort became even more boisterous; until even Betty was unable to tolerate him (Betty could generally tolerate ANY man). Marcia had, by now, lost count of how many times Mort had used "Good Lookin", "Young Lady" and "Sweet Young Thing" to address her. This really grated on Marcia's nerves. None of these were suitable "titles" for a freaking 50 year-old woman with streaks of gray running through her highlights. To make matters worse, Mort had gotten the impression that Marcia had "the hots" for him. Throughout the night, his polyester (confirmed) shirt had magically become unbuttoned even farther and Marcia shivered at the sight of his hairy, bear-like chest. "EEEEWWWWW, Betty, check it out!" Marcia exclaimed. "We have GOT to get out of here!"

Betty and Marcia hastily polished off their bottle of champagne and then made a low-profile exit through the side door. As they drove home, Marcia decided she was not feeling very optimistic about MWM making a marked difference in her life.

Now that Mort had Marcia's phone number, however, his incessant calls to Marcia began. Mort called Marcia on Tuesday night, Wednesday night, Thursday night and Friday night. Marcia could barely get through a two-minute phone conversation with Mort. Any guy who admitted he was "using the wrong part of his body" when he met his ex-wife really didn't stand a chance with Marcia. Any guy who sent Marcia TWO circus tickets in the mail–HINT, HINT–and then followed up with an awkward call every freaking evening obviously had some issues. Marcia did NOT like the circus–she thought it was cruel to abuse beautiful, innocent animals in such a fashion. The circus was NOT Marcia's idea of a good date. Marcia privately started to refer to Mort as "Mortifying Mort from MWM." Then things got even worse.

On Saturday, with the "Snow White and the Seven Dwarfs" soundtrack as sentimental (aka missing daughter-residing-in-Germany) background music, Marcia was frantically swiffering and dusting her collection of Russian nesting dolls. Marcia stepped out onto the front porch for a coffee break. It was a mild winter afternoon. Marcia heard a noise and looked up to see a large green John Deere lawnmower with an enormous snowplow attached, headed in her direction. Marcia did a double-take … it was freaking Mort on the lawn-plow! Mort, whom Marcia had been screening on Caller ID, in fact HIDING FROM, was almost to her front door! Stalking her, while using the lawn-plow as a decoy. Marcia was so shocked that she dropped her favorite green cappuccino cup, which shattered on the concrete stoop. Marcia ignored the broken shards and made a hasty retreat into her condo.

Once safely inside, Marcia shook her head in disbelief. First of all, she did not think it was even POSSIBLE to use a freaking John Deere tractor as a snowplow. Only thick-headed Mort could have devised this sort of scheme as a means of getting close to Marcia. Second of all, how did Mort even figure out where Marcia lived? Well, duh, Marcia realized, Mort had access to all MWM personal info and knew the area like the back of his hand. It didn't take a genius to see how Mort had finagled his way into Marcia-driveway-territory.

As it turned out, Mort had miraculously scored a maintenance job plowing snow at the Haystack Hills golf course, located directly across the street from Marcia's condo. Mort had eagerly accepted the job, knowing its proximity to Marcia's condo. Marcia was convinced, by this time, that Mort was "not right."

Mort spent the rest of that Saturday afternoon plowing the golf course grounds. Marcia spent the rest of that Saturday afternoon melting down at this invasion of privacy at her "DOLL HOUSE" condo. "There is no way in hell," Marcia thought, "no way in hell that MORT is going to be the first MALE guest in my sacred condo!" Not when her Daughter was gone, and certainly not when her Daughter was home. Even it if was on the pretense of being a "MWM bud." No way. This new Mort development did not lend itself to a variation on the tune "Set the Golf Course on Fire." Mort was falling hard and Marcia was running for the Haystack hills.

The bottom line was ... Marcia was TOO DAMN NICE! And, obviously a little "nice" was all Mort needed to fantasize that he and Marcia were going to be nominated MWM's Couple of the Year. Marcia could hear it now..."Presenting...Marcia and Mort, MWM's Prestigious Couple of the Year!" Marcia now needed to tell Mort "thank you for all your feedback and job-hunting support (and steak knife pitch, NOT) but I need some space right now." Marcia needed to QUIT BEING SO SPINELESS and tell Mort NOW so she would not have to endure the daily visual of Mort, lurking outside her condo in his sweat-stained, fur-trimmed parka and baggy, not-at-all-sexy track pants; his fur-lined (REAL fur, mind you!) leather cap with earflaps; his floppy, cracked Sorrell boots; and his oversized silver aviator-but-not-in a Brad-Pitt way sunglasses.

Later that afternoon, Mort casually loped his way across the now-plowed golf course parking lot to Marcia's front porch. Marcia saw him coming and hid in her large walk-in closet. Mort rang the doorbell repeatedly. Marcia cowered further under her black sequin dress. Mort finally gave up on the doorbell and stuck a Post-It note to Marcia's front door. Once Marcia had verified that the coast was clear, she retrieved the note. It read: "Hi Sweet Lips–just wanted to stop by for a glass of Martenelli's or a mug of hot chocolate...I'll call later. XO Mort." In Marcia's eyes, the note was Mort's lame attempt at humor (amore'). In Mort's eyes, it represented a witty "come-on." Marcia envisioned Mort's fleshy lips locking with her shapely lips and promptly made a mental note to double-lock all of her condo doors. And windows. She thought that Mort had, by now, gotten the hint but feared she must, instead, "undo" Mort before Mort did her in.

A few days later, Mort left a phone message to inform Marcia that he got fired from the Haystack Hills Golf Course after only two days–he had blown up the transmission on the John Deere lawn-plow. He was, however, already gainfully employed at Culver's. Did Marcia want to come and pick him up? He would treat her to a raspberry shake with his employee discount! "OMG," Marcia groaned, "does it EVER end?" Marcia's hopes of finding a worthy BOY-FOR-THE-WINTER were rapidly diminishing.

MARCH 3–WEDNESDAY
DAYS TILL MUSIC CRUISE=11
DAYS SINCE PROMISE OF CALL FROM IRISH=37
MARCIA'S BEVVIE-OF-THE-MOMENT=BAILEY'S ON THE ROCKS THE SIZE OF EAST TEXAS
BRANDI'S LYRICS (VIA HEADPHONES) THAT GET HER THRU=IN A CROWDED ROOM, I'M ALONE

Marcia had, at that point, used up her FLAME.com 30-day trial to no avail. It took less than thirty days to determine that there was not a single man on FLAME.com that would "get" her anyway. Marcia moved waaaaay too fast for the FLAME.com male mentality. Besides, the thought of yet ANOTHER BLIND DATE was more than Marcia could bear.

Marcia decided to take a different approach and create a profile on a social networking site to see if she could re-connect with a man she actually KNEW. Betty had once recommended FACESPACE.COM as a site that Marcia could use to start re-connecting. Marcia was skeptical. She could think of only a handful of men from her past (high school and/or college) that she would be interested in looking up. To do so, Marcia would need to reallocate her FLAME.com hours to FACESPACE.COM hours. This did not mean she could turn into a "loose cannon" on FACESPACE.COM, and spend all her free time chatting with acquaintances from thirty years ago, while her whisk sales floundered. Nor could Marcia while away her precious free time playing video-type FACESPACE.COM games. Marcia was, in fact, embarking on a FACESPACE.COM "man mission"–she just hadn't realized it yet.

MARCH 5–FRIDAY
DAYS TILL MUSIC CRUISE=9
DAYS SINCE PROMISE OF CALL FROM IRISH=39
MARCIA'S BEVVIE-OF-THE-MOMENT = STARBUCKS CAPPUCINO PRIMO MADE IN HER NEW COFFEEMAKER
BRANDI'S LYRICS (VIA HEADPHONES) THAT GET HER THRU=YOU CAN'T BREAK A HEART THAT WASN'T EVEN YOURS TO BREAK

Marcia spent her entire day Friday at home, reviewing photos her daughter had taken of her earlier that year for her FLAME.com profile. Marcia now had to choose the most flattering of these photos to post on her FACESPACE.COM profile in order to impress her former male colleagues. One photo, in particular, stood out as "THE" photo to use. It captured Marcia in her short, sassy 'do, wearing a simple grey, ruffle-necked Henley and her oversized "H-I-T-H-T winnings" gold earrings. It would do for her main profile photo.

Marcia logged on to FACESPACE.COM and created a bare-bones profile in record time. Details such as links to her favorite song websites or "likes and dislikes" on her profile would have to wait. Marcia had NO TIME for this! Her name, location and photos would have to suffice for now. The music cruise was a mere nine days away and Marcia needed to find a potential cruise cabin mate, ha-ha! Heck, she had attended a high school with a population of 3,000 students. The odds of reconnecting with a man on FACESPACE.COM had to be better than scouring strangers on FLAME.com! At least men from her past already know how she "worked", personality-wise. Marcia was very excited to see exactly WHO from high school or college might have a profile on FACESPACE.COM. However, in her usual disciplined manner, she decided to hold off. She could wait until her allotted "browse break" aka "honcho hour" the next morning to log on to FACESPACE.COM. It would give her something to look forward to.

Marcia would not abuse her free time that morning by lollygagging online. Instead, she would whip her condo into spotless condition. Marcia could then simultaneously process "Mort Madness", as she and Betty called it. She would multi-task, as usual. Mort must be purged from her system. Marcia, once again, felt SO DONE WITH DATING and needed to refresh her heart before venturing on. Marcia knew she must approach

FACESPACE.COM with EXTREME CAUTION. While vigorously scrubbing kitchen counters, Marcia made a promise to herself not to let ANY FACESPACE.COM man trample on her heart. Marcia's previous dating experience had started to pay off, if only in this respect.

MARCH 7–SUNDAY
DAYS TILL MUSIC CRUISE=7
DAYS SINCE PROMISE OF CALL FROM IRISH=41
MARCIA'S BEVVIE-OF-THE-MOMENT=BAILEY'S ON THE ROCKS THE SIZE OF EAST TEXAS
BRANDI'S LYRICS (VIA HEADPHONES) THAT GET HER THRU=I'M HAPPY CAN'T YOU SEE, I'M ALRIGHT

Marcia's first round on FACESPACE.COM was somewhat rewarding. She was able to "be-friend" several old gal pals, as well as a few ancient high school "flames." Marcia was so encouraged by her growing group of "friends" that she broke her profile review rules and stayed logged on to FACESPACE.COM all that week. On her second FACESPACE.COM round, Marcia sent a "friend" request to an old neighbor named Tommy. Surprisingly, it only took Tommy two days to acknowledge Marcia's friend request. There was even a brief accompanying message "Hey, Marcia! What's new? You look GREAT!" Marcia was touched by Tommy's friendly message. She recalled sharing many a beer at high school keggers in the woods with Tommy. Tommy had been a popular, witty guy in high school and his current FACESPACE.COM photos indicated that this had probably not changed much in his adult life.

Marcia had, by now, figured out how to view friends OF friends on FACESPACE.COM and, on an impulse, decided to scroll through Tommy's vast group of friend photos. One, in particular, caught her eye. It was a photo of Rodney, another old neighbor of hers. Marcia literally screamed "OMG, RODNEY…!" when she realized it was him in the photo. She could not help but smile back at his photo…it was sooooooo cute!

The photo showed Rodney on a red, rocky cliff with an enormous lake in the background and the sun setting in the distance. He was dressed in a crisp button down shirt and jeans and sandals. Marcia could not take her eyes off Rodney's photo. She pretty much melted into a pool of desire right then and there.

However, she did not know how FACESPACE.COM operated. Could Rodney virtually tell that she was stalking his profile pic? Marcia made a hasty decision to do what she always did in this situation–right-click on the photo and hastily copy it into a Word document. That way, she could see Rodney's amazing, handsome face any time she wanted to! Without fear of getting caught committing any FACESPACE.COM crimes! It was brilliant! Rodney would never suspect that an ex-neighbor was literally drooling over him on FACESPACE.COM. Marcia returned to Rodney's photo countless times that week, during coffee breaks at the Whisks R Us warehouse. It helped her get through the monotonous working days.

Marcia then decided she would be extremely BOLD and write Rodney a message via FACESPACE.COM. It took her four hours to formulate the right words. She hoped her words conveyed a breezy, confident tone. She also hoped Rodney would not be alarmed that she was up to anything other than saying "HI" to an old high school pal.

What Marcia did not realize was that, on FACESPACE.COM, she had to become a friend of Rodney's before she could actually send him her carefully composed message. Well, Marcia, thought, a friend request from Rodney should be easy enough to get. If Tommy had friend-ed her, SURELY Rodney would do the same? She may as well take the leap. What was the worst thing that could happen? Why the hell was Marcia so NERVOUS about sending Rodney a simple electronic friend request? Would Rodney REJECT her friend request? How could he do that to Marcia? Rodney had NO FREAKING CLUE that Marcia had feelings for him. Rodney was her old NEIGHBOR, for crying out loud. Marcia continued to ponder every possible reason Rodney might have to reject her. This took a full six hours. Once Marcia had narrowed rejection reasons down to only ONE (the time she threw up on Rodney's feet at a mutual friend's alcohol-infused party), she sent the request to Rodney. The "friend request" waiting game had begun.

MARCH 8–MONDAY
DAYS TILL MUSIC CRUISE=6
DAYS SINCE PROMISE OF CALL FROM IRISH=42
DAYS SINCE FRIEND REQUEST SENT TO RODNEY=1
**MARCIA'S BEVVIE-OF-THE-MOMENT = STARBUCKS
CAPPUCINO PRIMO MADE IN HER NEW COFFEEMAKER;
BAILEY'S ON THE ROCKS THE SIZE OF EAST TEXAS**
BRANDI'S LYRICS (VIA HEADPHONES) THAT GET HER
THRU=YOU CAN'T BREAK A HEART THAT WASN'T EVEN
YOURS TO BREAK

At 4:00 A.M. the next morning (in order to avoid site "traffic"), Marcia logged on to FACESPACE.COM. Marcia felt a burning desire to scrutinize Rodney's profile to see if she could glean any more info. Ironically, Rodney's FACESPACE.COM profile read like an open book. Marcia was privy to all KINDS of information. Rodney was only selective, setting-wise, about who could actually CONTACT him. As it turned out, looking at Rodney's profile was NOT a good idea.

Marcia was quickly able to determine that Rodney had 156 female friends. Female friends that Marcia did not think she could hold a candle to, looks-wise. In fact, Rodney's female friend photos looked like they all came fresh off the cover of Glamour or Vogue. Perfectly coiffed and lipsticked. Hell, Marcia had worn lipstick three times since high school. Zero times IN high school. Also, Marcia CHOSE to dress in brightly-colored PJ pants patterned in rainbow-striped deer-donning-scarves. She CHOSE to wear no bra versus a sexy scarlet brassiere with matching be-ribboned panties. She CHOSE to wear pink "run-away" Mary Jane shoes. She even CHOSE to apply mascara only if it was a good day. How could Marcia EVER stack up to the Rodney "friend" competition? How could Marcia, who shopped at Target for cruise wear, ever be a contender with women whose shoes looked like they cost six times Marcia's entire cruise wear budget?

Marcia was extremely depressed. Marcia was NOT a jet-setter. To her credit, Marcia had a great sense of humor and adventure. And she HAD traveled throughout Europe several times. Marcia had dined on escargot in Paris and sipped local wine at well-known wineries in Spain. But Marcia knew that she would never be the kind of woman who bought True Religion jeans, or who wore heels higher than .5 inches. Marcia would ALWAYS be a simple, down-to-earth girl. Chin up, Bucky, Marcia reminded herself, YOU ARE A VERY GOOD CATCH! Do not let yourself be intimidated by FACESPACE.COM profile photos.

Marcia sighed and went to add a dollop of Bailey's to her coffee. Bailey's in her 4 A.M. coffee might help make her feel better. NO WONDER Rodney was not "clearing" her FACESPACE.COM friend request. Rodney had become a FREAKING PLAYER! It was obvious that his photo was being "right-clicked on" by women world-wide!

Marcia needed to decide how long she should wait for Rodney to reply to her simple friend request. Would Marcia ultimately have to settle for Irish Bun's mediocre kisses instead of Rodney's? Not that Marcia had ANY clue what kind of a kisser Rodney was anyway. There were instances where the most suave, most "right-clicked" man ended up being worthless, tongue-wise. Marcia clicked over to her photo of Rodney to inspect his lips. This told her nothing. Marcia poured herself three more shots of Bailey's (sans coffee) in quick succession. Based on the woman "latched onto" Rodney's profile, Marcia intuited that Rodney was an excellent kisser. When, Marcia wondered, would she ever find a man who was her match, kissing-wise?

Marcia picked up the phone and scheduled, in the following order: a haircut, highlights, manicure, pedicure, cellulite-reduction therapy and a sea-salt full body scrub. Her voice was, by this time, slightly slurred. Her means of paying for these services were none. But Marcia did not give a rip. She was going to prep for the POSSIBILITY of a friend request approval from Rodney. And, if nothing else, she would be ready for the cruise.

MARCH 10–WEDNESDAY
DAYS TILL MUSIC CRUISE=4
DAYS SINCE PROMISE OF CALL FROM IRISH=44
DAYS SINCE FRIEND REQUEST SENT TO RODNEY=5
**MARCIA'S BEVVIE-OF-THE-MOMENT=STRONG FRENCH
ROAST WITH 1/2 & 1/2**
BRANDI'S LYRICS (VIA HEADPHONES) THAT GET HER
THRU=I'M HAPPY CAN'T YOU SEE, I'M ALRIGHT

Marcia had, by now, become quite proficient on FACESPACE.COM.
She had done so by devoting her early morning hours before work to
FACESPACE.COM. This morning, she had spent time online adding
info to her profile and answering FACESPACE.COM correspondence.
FACESPACE.COM provided Marcia with an easy way to stay in touch
with her close female friends, while reuniting with old ones.

Marcia true friends not only cared about Marcia but they also WORRIED
about Marcia's lengthy "single" status. Marcia's "CRY WOLF" dating stories
(aka "I'VE FINALLY FOUND THE ONE") were seemingly endless. Such
stories provided Marcia's friends with much-needed DRAMA. Sometimes
more drama than any of them could ask for. Marcia was notorious for
making up date story happy endings – even after only one date with a
man. Her pals had endured "CRY WOLF" Marcia stories for years. Not
only were they ALWAYS there to pick up the pieces when Marcia's date
stories had an unhappy outcome, Marcia's pals were ALWAYS there to tell
her what to do in "real life."

So it was natural, now that Marcia was writing a blockbuster novel aka
screenplay, that Marcia's friends wanted to know how the ending turned
out in her novel. Even if her book had a "CRY WOLF" ending. Marcia's
FACESPACE.COM friends were begging Marcia to "TELL ALL." The
level of excitement on FACESPACE.COM was quite high - it was now up
to Marcia to provide some "site drama."

Several of these same enthusiastic pals had even WRITTEN sample
book endings and sent them to Marcia. In fact, Marcia was overwhelmed
with a flood of sample book "ENDINGS" in her FACESPACE.COM
inbox. Marcia wondered if any of the sample book "ENDINGS" from
her pals were their "real life" advice for her disguised as "fiction." Marcia

chuckled—some of her friends had pretty wild imaginations. She decided that her friends were simply trying to help "further the cause." After all, almost EVERY woman she knew could relate to dating sagas. Even if (as in Marcia's case) they were only fiction.

Having given in to peer pressure, Marcia decided to post her book ending snippet right then and there on her FACESPACE.COM profile. Marcia had only a few minutes until work time began. She quickly uploaded the file, titled "PINK.ROC.DOC", to her profile. Posting "PINK.ROC. DOC" was the most EFFICIENT way to let all her friends know how her novel ended in one fell sweep. Those friends that did not yet want to hear the ending could simply not read it. Marcia had worked very hard on her novel and her idea for the ending was one of her favorite parts. Marcia was fairly certain she would get LOTS of feedback on the novel ending from her pals. It would be up to Marcia's pals to decide if the ending smacked of "CRY WOLF."

Once she had posted her "PINK.ROC.DOC" snippet, Marcia breathed a sigh of relief. It would take some time before her pals all read her updated FACESPACE.COM profile. Marcia had NO MORE TIME to spend lollygagging on FACESPACE.COM. She must get back to her Whisk Work Week and look ahead to her upcoming music cruise.

MARCH 12–FRIDAY
DAYS TILL MUSIC CRUISE=2
DAYS SINCE PROMISE OF CALL FROM IRISH=46
DAYS SINCE FRIEND REQUEST SENT TO RODNEY=8
MARCIA'S BEVVIE-OF-THE-MOMENT=STRONG FRENCH ROAST WITH 1/2 & 1/2
BRANDI'S LYRICS (VIA HEADPHONES) THAT GET HER THRU=YOU CAN'T BREAK A HEART THAT WASN'T EVEN YOURS TO BREAK

A few days later, Marcia sat in the Whisks R Us warehouse, newly shorn and highlighted and scrubbed and de-cellulite-ed. Yet even with her massive makeover, looking absolutely fantastic in her black ruffled sweater and sparkly semi-precious stone necklace with the sexy back-of-neck-extension, Marcia was still blue. She wished, with all her heart, it had been Rodney who had responded to her FACESPACE.COM request instead of Tommy. In fact, Marcia had gotten several male friend requests since she had sent one to Rodney. Marcia had even posted new, improved photos on her FACESPACE.COM profile to try and turn up the heat and MAKE RODNEY NOTICE HER. Of all her high school pals, RODNEY was forefront in Marcia's mind.

To make matters worse, Marcia had a dream about Rodney that very morning. The first feeling she had, upon awakening, was one of being completely wrapped in Rodney's arms. This was not some made-up fantasy like Marcia usually concocted. This was a freaking Cayamo blankie safe and warm feeling. In the dream, Rodney had been standing behind Marcia with his arms encircling her as they stood near the seashore. This luscious dream only made Marcia feel worse. Why was she tormented so by Rodney? Why hadn't he responded to her? Marcia doubted she would ever "stack up" against Rodney's vast list of female friends, except maybe in the breast department.

Marcia sighed and applied Rosemary oil so that she could get back to her monster Excel whisk sales spread sheet calculations. But not even Rosemary oil was helping her to focus. Marcia was too distracted by sad thoughts of Rodney. She knew immediately how to solve this dilemma. Marcia needed to cut out early and PLAY HOOKEY! Marcia promptly packed up her freaking Excel spreadsheets and hit the open road to Haystack in her Hybrid. Driving on the empty WI back roads and singing to her cranked-up stereo was a sure-fire way to combat the blues. Once Marcia got to Haystack, she could begin another project - PACKING HER SUITCASES! Her long-awaited music cruise was only TWO days away. Packing required little thought, which provided relief for her over-worked brain. Packing was therapeutic.

Later that evening, Marcia glanced around her bedroom. It looked as though a tornado had swept through it. Clothing was stacked on her bed, miscellaneous bathing suit bottoms were strewn around, bags of sunscreen and toiletries sat atop every surface. Marcia NEVER got the three-ounce carry-on rule for the airplane right. She VOWED that this year she was going to purchase quart size plastic bags, not gallon size. Then she was going to measure all toiletries into three-ounce containers and GET THE FREAKING TOILETRIES THROUGH TO THE PLANE so that she actually had sunscreen and shampoo and moisturizer at her disposal on the ship.

Marcia had, however, momentarily been distracted by a fleeting thought of Rodney. Only because a sweet, sad song came on the radio while she was haphazardly stuffing items into her suitcase. Marcia stopped with a start, realizing it had now been EIGHT long days since she had sent her FACESPACE.COM friend request. And not one peep from Rodney. The heartbreaking song, combined with this realization, nearly brought Marcia to tears. Why, why, why did Marcia have such horrible luck with men? It was bad enough that Marcia could not find a man brave enough to date her. Marcia had now reached an all-time low—she could not even get Rodney to "friend" her.

Marcia shook her head to quickly clear it of such a depressing thought. What the hell was she doing, sobbing over a sappy song on the radio and a cute guy she had known 32 years earlier? This was supposed to be a HAPPY, EXCITING countdown to her relaxing cruise. She had NO TIME for getting her head stuck in the past. She had no time to get caught up in the FACESPACE.COM craze. She had no time to be carefully studying every freaking photo Rodney had posted on his FACESPACE.COM profile.

Unfortunately for Marcia, spending countless hours studying Rodney photos was exactly what she HAD been doing on FACESPACE.COM over the past eight days. This was not entirely her fault. Rodney had FORTY-FOUR FREAKING PHOTO ALBUMS on his profile to peruse. Marcia could not help that Rodney had posted forty-four photo scrapbooks. "Local" scrapbooks that contained photos of Rodney walking in peak autumn-foliage forests or snowshoeing by candlelight at his up-north WI hideaway. "Travel" scrapbooks that contained photos not only of gorgeous exotic locales, but that revealed Rodney in said exotic locales surrounded by members of his 156 female FACESPACE.COM "harem!" Female "friends" attired in teensy bikinis (bikinis that Marcia could not even squeeze one boob into, let alone a thigh) or gorgeous flowing summery dresses. Obviously, Marcia had to inspect EVERY FREAKING RODNEY PHOTO on FACESPACE.COM to try and determine if Rodney was indeed "A PLAYER" or not.

Marcia, however, had MUCH bigger priorities than melting down over Rodney and his heart-wrenching travel photos. Betty had supplied Marcia with new, top-of-the-line catheter bags to fill with tequila so that Marcia could sneak alcohol on the cruise. Marcia had calculated that one-quarter of her suitcase would need to be packed with the catheter bags in order to enjoy tasty margaritas on the ship. So that she would not rack up a $1,000 drink bill while cruising. Marcia needed to figure out the best way to weave the catheter bags into various articles of clothing so as not to get them confiscated at the Port of Miami. She remembered seeing the enormous pile of assorted liquor bottles that had gotten taken away last year as cruise guests boarded the ship. Marcia was confident that Betty's method of smuggling tequila would be a success.

MARCH 14–SUNDAY
DAYS TILL MUSIC CRUISE = 0
DAYS SINCE PROMISE OF CALL FROM IRISH=48
DAYS SINCE FRIEND REQUEST SENT TO RODNEY=9
MARCIA'S BEVVIE-OF-THE-MORNING=CAFFE CON LECHE, SLIGHTLY SWEETENED
MARCIA'S BEVVIE-OF-THE-AFTERNOON=CHAMPAGNE UPON BOARDING THE CRUISE SHIP
BRANDI'S LYRICS (VIA HEADPHONES) THAT GET HER THRU=I'M HAPPY CAN'T YOU SEE, I'M ALRIGHT

Marcia was currently near Biscayne Bay in Miami on a gorgeous Sunday morning. Sitting at a little café table by the marina, people-watching. It was a bit windy off the water but Marcia was enjoying her absolute favorite BEVVIE OF THE DAY–cafe con leche! She had ordered it sweetened (just a tad) because she was on VACATION! Her cruise ship was leaving in six hours! She could relax by the water for a while and then she had to go pack up her bags in the best possible fashion for efficient ship-boarding. She looked somewhat dork-ish in her Cayamo T-shirt with large headphones clamped to her head. But she really did not give a rip–the Marriott Biscayne Bay employees would not be seeing her again, or for another year, anyway.

The front desk employees had been very friendly and accommodating the previous night when Marcia had finally arrived at the Marriott, weary after a long travel day from WI. However, because Marcia's room had been, at that moment (1:30 freaking A.M.!) being cleaned, she had not been able to indulge in the long, hot shower she had anticipated immediately upon arrival. Because of this inconvenience, the sweet woman at the front desk had stowed Marcia's luggage AND given her a yellow ticket, which entitled Marcia to two free margaritas! Marcia LOVED freebies on vacation–frankly, she was a little bit out of her league, budget-wise, at the Marriott.

Marcia had promptly taken her free drink coupons to the hotel bar to redeem since there was only fifteen minutes left until closing time. The atmosphere in the bar was a little too intense for Marcia–the barstools were occupied by young, drunken, obnoxious men and women from a wedding party. One of the "schnibbied" men had been yelling loudly across the bar about f------ women. Marcia had been insulted by this behavior. She had hoped to meet up with her fellow cruise pals at the bar that evening but had arrived at the hotel much too late.

Marcia left the bar and went outside to sit on a beech wood bench in the smoking area and savor the warm Florida midnight air. While drinking her second complimentary margarita (feeling, by now, a bit tipsy), she had conversed with a very nice, wise female high school teacher from Florida. The teacher had been staying at the hotel for a few nights and was traveling the next day on a private jet! up through Florida, and then further north to the Carolinas. Marcia was impressed. Once the nice teacher had bid her "Good night" and departed, Marcia sat alone, fantasizing about what it would be like to meet people who owned private jets. People who would invite Marcia to join them on their private jet travels. Marcia quickly chastised herself for such foolish thoughts—she had no time for private jet travel anyway. She was fortunate enough to be leaving on her favorite music cruise in just a matter of hours!

As predicted, an escape to a warmer climate was proving to be just what the doctor ordered for Marcia. The ocean, the palm trees, the sunshine warming her face that morning, the brightly-colored foliage, the delicious cafe con leche—all of these things allowed Marcia to immediately forget about the horrendous winter back in Haystack.
Marcia applied another coat of sunscreen to her face and decided to place one last call to her friend Betty so that she could share the beauty of the Miami day with her. Marcia picked up her cell phone and dialed Betty's number—but the call would not go through. Marcia took this as a sign that she should not return, in any sense, to the world of Haystack. The fact that she was unable to contact her friend in Wisconsin simply confirmed that she was now OFFICIALLY ON VACATION! She was no longer accountable to ANYONE! This was Marcia's favorite "status." Betty would just have to wait to hear about Marcia's adventures upon her return to Haystack.

Marcia lit up another cig (riiiiight) to enjoy with the remainder of her cafe con leche. She felt very lucky, and grateful, to embark on this adventure. She also felt a bit sleep-deprived because she had been too excited to sleep more than three hours the night before. But it did not matter. Her face already felt like it had color after only fifteen minutes in the Miami sun.

The warm wind was blowing through her hair, which meant her new highlights were going to turn even blonder. It was such a happy morning. Marcia realized she was sitting at "lucky" Pier #4, which was a great way to start her day. She watched a "Monster fishing boat" slowly leave the pier, making its daily ocean run. Marcia could not wait until the moment her cruise ship, too, left the pier. She belonged on the ocean. There was no better feeling in the world than being onboard a boat and watching the land slip away.

Marcia decided she had better quit daydreaming and go finish packing. Her feet were getting sunburned. Marcia needed to preserve her feet for wild dancing on the ship. All she had to do now was finish re-packing her luggage and get herself to the Port of Miami.

MARCH 15–MONDAY
DAYS ON! MUSIC CRUISE=1
DAYS SINCE PROMISE OF CALL FROM IRISH=UNKNOWN–
MARCIA HAD LOST COUNT AND THERE WAS NO PHONE
SERVICE ON SHIP
DAYS SINCE FRIEND REQUEST SENT TO RODNEY=UNKNOWN.
MARCIA HAD LOST COUNT AND HER SELF-IMPOSED SHIP
RULE WAS NO CHECKING E-MAIL OR FACESPACE.COM
**MARCIA'S BEVVIE-OF-THE-MOMENT = CRUISE SHIP
CAPPICINO, FROSTY MARGARITAS**
BRANDI'S LYRICS (VIA HEADPHONES) THAT GET HER
THRU=I'M HAPPY CAN'T YOU SEE, I'M ALRIGHT

Her first morning on the cruise, Marcia was up at 6:00 AM, anxious to snag a chaise lounge on the swimming pool deck and soak up some sun. Rumor had it that there could potentially be pool deck chaise lounge wars between cruise guests. It was thus imperative for Marcia to rise at dawn in order to secure a chaise lounge. Marcia's beach bag contained the essentials–a bottle of sunscreen (70 proof), a racy novel, and a beach cover-up to monitor her allotment of sun. The ocean-filled sky was perfectly clear. Marcia did not want to get sunburned beyond recognition on her first day.

Once Marcia had enjoyed her morning cappuccino, she switched up her "bevvie of the day" to a slushy, vodka-infused, cherry limeade. It was the perfect drink to celebrate the ship having left the Port of Miami behind. The ship had been cruising rapidly through the welcoming azure ocean all night. Granted, 8:00 A.M. was a TAD early for alcohol but it was Marcia's freaking vacation! For the foreseeable future, time no longer had any meaning! Marcia could drink WHATEVER SHE WANTED. She was accountable to NO ONE! Once Marcia had sucked down her cherry limeade, the friendly bartender next recommended a "Miami Vice", which translated to a pina colada topped off with half-and-half and Blue Curacao. It was garnished with a chunk of fresh pineapple, a maraschino cherry and a festive paper umbrella. In cruise terms, this drink could almost qualify as breakfast.

Marcia had to be careful to monitor the number of "umbrella drinks" she consumed that morning. Too many drinks too early in the day meant danger, danger. Marcia did not want to end up "under the table" at lunchtime. Rather, Marcia wanted to be dancing ON the table with a lampshade on her head when the open-air music began later that day. Marcia refrained from consuming additional umbrella bevvies so as to enjoy the day and the music and the social time with people from ALL OVER THE U.S. AND BEYOND!

The setup of the ship's pool deck was conducive to drinking and sunning and swimming and hot tubbing and listening to amazing live bands that performed all day under an aqua and white striped awning. Gallons of sunscreen would be applied by guests. The Tahitian salt water swimming pools and hot tubs were surrounded by enormous palm tree lamps that lit up after sunset. Sadly, half of the hot tubs had to be drained so that the water wouldn't ruin the sound equipment. However, if you were an early riser like Marcia, you could start each day with a relaxing hot tub to ease aching, over-danced muscles. Some guests even enjoyed concerts while soaking in the hot tubs. Any and all seats on the pool deck were utilized.

A long bar stood at one end of the pool deck. Beer and Cosmos and cherry limeades and pinot grigio and tall, frozen margaritas and pina coladas were served at the swim deck bar from 7 A.M. to midnight.

The bar stools were painted in bright pastel colors and were quickly snatched up by some of the more colorful characters on the cruise. Because of this, standing in line at the bar could lead to some pretty interesting conversation.

Marcia preferred to keep a low profile early in the day. She had met up with some past-year cruise pals who would be joining her shortly on the sun deck. She had, in fact, saved her cruise gal pals chaise lounges by "marking" them with her sandals and beach towel. As the day went on, she and her pals would get progressively wilder, depending on what band was currently playing. Marcia hoped all of them would soon be letting down their hair and dancing on the sun deck. Marcia loved to dance.

For now, Marcia was content to sprawl on her chaise lounge and savor the feeling of warm sun on her sun block-slathered face. From time to time, Marcia would seek shelter in the shade. Marcia's idea of morning exercise on the ship was running up and down the nearby flight of stairs to the shaded smoking area. Marcia could have easily slipped into her tennis shoes and racing bra and power-walked around the ship on the specially designed walking track instead. In fact, Marcia had purchased new "Shape Up" sneakers expressly for this purpose. Marcia had made a vow to try and change some of her bad ship habits. But, in Marcia's mind, ship power-walking was NOT a sanctioned VACATION activity! Therefore, Marcia had purposely left her brand new Shape Up sneakers AT HOME in their box to ensure she would NOT use the walking track. Walking was work and Marcia had no time for work, only play, on the cruise.

The designated smoking area featured festive hot pink and lime green tables and comfortable cushion-back chairs. It took up one-half of the ship's shaded deck and was tucked one level below the sun deck. The smoking section was a place where an artist-wanna-be, such as Marcia, would hang out (versus the non-smoking section, where the more health-conscious guests lounged). A pipe smoker and a cigar smoker were sitting at the table next to Marcia. There was also a table nearby, surrounded by what looked like cruise musicians. They stood out, because of their unique, NY-style hats and all-black clothing and "special" Cayamo key cards. One of the musicians wore black, "red-eyed" high top sneakers—only the top lace hole of the high top was red. Oftentimes, cruise musician's eyes were red as well. Some bands on the music cruise were known to perform an evening set that ended up lasting well into the wee hours of the morning. Big, dark sunglasses were a dead giveaway when attempting to identify which guests were, in fact, rock stars.

Marcia's cruise pals teased her because she was always looking for an "autograph op" with the rock stars on the ship. Being a diehard fan of so many of the bands on board, Marcia had prepped for "auto-ops" by packing CD covers for each of her favorite bands to autograph. The previous year, Marcia had used the Cayamo promo CD to get as many autographs as possible. This year, Marcia was going to use her sunhat and a borrowed purple Sharpie as a means of capturing autographs. Marcia's pals thought she was a nut. Marcia did not care—getting autographs was a perfect way to create happy memories. Besides, the same pals who gave her a hard time had been known to snatch "set lists" from the stage after one of THEIR favorite artists performed on-ship. Marcia preferred hastily scribbled, illegible purple sharpie signatures to typed set lists. In the end, only one thing really mattered—Marcia and her pals lived for the music.

Marcia had group-nicknamed her cruise pals the "Cayamo Cay-gals" vs. Cowgirls. Like Marcia, they understood the importance of nicknames and already had nicknames of their own. Nicknames such as Luscious Brown (aka Precious Brown) and Jilly and Jem. Marcia shortened these nicknames to PB & J & J (peanut butter and jelly and jelly).

Marcia and the "Cayamo Cay-gals" were a force to be reckoned with. Luscious Brown was known for her ability to keep a mean tambourine beat. Her goal was to score a "sit in" with any or all of the bands performing on the cruise. Jilly was known to use phrases like "well, butter my butt and call me a biscuit" and donned an awesome red cowgirl hat. Jilly already had stage experience; she played a wicked cow bell in her rock star boyfriend's band. Jilly, therefore, did not have the same burning desire for a "sit in" as Luscious Brown. Jem aka Gem had both piano and percussion experience. And Marcia had years of acoustic guitar lessons under her belt, although her repertoire was limited to exactly three songs. After hours of sun and fun (aka cold beer and cigarettes), the four of them joked that they could sign up for a slot at the "Open Mic" contest on the ship. Marcia secretly did not like this idea—she suffered from horrible stage fright ever since her minor singing role as a baker in the high school performance of "Oliver."

Marcia knew, however, that ANYTHING was possible when it came to the "Cayamo Cay-gals." Marcia was already a bit nervous about their scheduled excursion to the "Doused Dollar" beach bar the very next day. It was their first port of call and the "Cayamo Cay-gals" had invited Marcia to join them at the "Doused." The excursion was touted as such: the women would board a catamaran from the cruise ship. The catamaran would take them to a beautiful private island that sported a beach bar with a thatched palm frond roof, loud beach-y music and all-you-could-drink rum punch. Also included in the price of the excursion were miniature bottles of A) Category Two Hurricane Hot Peppa Sauce, complete with a matching miniature straw hat perched jauntily on its' "head" and B) award-winning St. Croix Cruzan Banana Rum. The one of a kind "Doused Dollar Day" was sure to be an adventure.

The first day on the cruise continued to pass in a glorious haze of music and bevvies and laughter and casino roulette and dancing. There were also trips to the buffet to refuel for more dancing. Marcia's high-end apple green sandals proved to be worth every penny. Although she did not dance ON a table with a lampshade on her head, she was still dancing when the palm tree lamps began to glow. There was nothing but ocean views surrounding the dance floor, which led to a "no-boundaries" kind of feeling for both the band members and their fans. There was no curfew, either, but the Cay-gals knew it was best to retire to their cabins at a reasonable hour that night (a reasonable hour, in cruise terms, meant anytime before 5 A.M.). Their "Doused Dollar" adventure started early the next morning, but all of the women knew that lounging on a gorgeous beach would require absolutely no effort on their part. This was one of the biggest perks of being on vacation.

MARCH 16–TUESDAY
DAYS ON MUSIC CRUISE=2
DAYS SINCE PROMISE OF CALL FROM IRISH=UNKNOWN–
MARCIA HAD LOST COUNT AND THERE WAS NO PHONE
SERVICE ON SHIP
DAYS SINCE FRIEND REQUEST SENT TO RODNEY=UNKNOWN.
MARCIA HAD LOST COUNT AND HER SELF-IMPOSED SHIP
RULE WAS NO CHECKING E-MAIL OR FACESPACE.COM
**MARCIA'S BEVVIE-OF-THE-MOMENT=PAINKILLERS AND
"DOUSED" RUM PUNCH**
BRANDI'S LYRICS (VIA HEADPHONES) THAT GET HER
THRU=I'M HAPPY CAN'T YOU SEE, I'M ALRIGHT

The next morning Marcia awoke and opened her porthole window curtains to get a peek at the sun rising on the white-capped water. It was an amazing sight–another perfect day had begun. Marcia was fortunate enough to have a cabin with a porthole, even though the bottom half of her view was a large lifeboat tethered to the outside wall. Other guests that had booked "inside" cabins were not as lucky. There was a much better chance of feeling seasick when there were no windows in the cabin to orient the occupants. Marcia remembered hearing some horrific "inside room" seasickness tales the previous year. Seasickness was not a good sensation to experience with a tummy full of beer and margaritas. Marcia had heard a story about a drunken guest who had unfortunately scored top bunk sleeping privileges. In the middle of the night, the guest was "thrown off" her bunk directly onto her roommate below, along with her tummy full of beer and margaritas. Not a happy cabin memory. Marcia had no such worries. Marcia NEVER got seasick, even when the ocean waves were noticeable enough to make the rock stars sway on the stage.

Marcia now needed to quit lollygagging and get ready to meet her pals for their expedition. The catamaran was leaving to the "Doused Dollar" in one half hour. It was easy to get ready for a day on the beach – all she needed was a swimming suit and flip-flops. No mascara was necessary. Marcia ruffled her bed-head hair and was out the cabin door in a matter of minutes.

Up on the smoking deck, the women buzzed with caffeine and excitement. Luscious Brown (aka PB) was already in fine form, teasing Marcia about her big, floppy, dorky, autographed sunhat and modest swimsuit cover-up. PB & J & J could suntan until they were the color of mahogany without consequence. Fair-skinned Marcia, who hardly ever even saw the sun during a Wisconsin winter, would instantly go into sun overload status. Marcia was fine with the idea of a handsome fellow cruiser having to carry her back onboard from the "Doused Dollar" that day, but she would prefer that her unconscious state would be caused by rum overload, not sun overload. Besides, Marcia did not care if she looked silly in her sunhat–the "Doused Dollar" was a silly place! Marcia would fit right in! Marcia was especially looking forward to sipping a famous "Painkiller" with lots of nutmeg on top–it would help to counteract the margaritas from the night before.

The women located their catamaran and boarded, crowding onto a wooden bench. Luscious, her lips outlined perfectly in pink gloss, boarded the boat with a flourish. She addressed the cute catamaran captain as "Big Daddy" and boldly gave him a kiss. The captain blushed and, in return, gave Luscious the honor of sharing the captain's chair with him for the duration of the ride. Marcia could not help but laugh at Luscious' boldness–she attracted men so effortlessly. Marcia vowed to learn a few tricks from her.

Some of the guests on board were quickly downing Bloody Marys in preparation for the beach bar. It was an "all you could drink" rum punch day, not to be wasted due to lingering hangovers. A man sitting nearby regaled the four women with legendary wild boar tales from the island. He warned the women not to stray too far from the "Doused" itself - an inebriated guest had been bored by a boar and had needed seventeen stitches the previous year. Marcia and her pals listened, wide-eyed, to the story and quickly made a pact to travel in pairs should they decide to explore the island's outer limits.

The catamaran was forced to drop Marcia and her pals a short distance from the island. It was up to them to navigate through the beautiful Caribbean waters to the beach. The four women felt happy and carefree. The salty water was so warm and inviting that they ended up riding the waves to the beach, hoping their cigarettes, encased in a gallon sized baggie, would stay dry. Marcia never realized until that moment how much she loved to submerge her head in the ocean. It was so different from the sterile hotel pool she sometimes used back in Wisconsin. None of the women cared if they arrived at the bar soaking wet. This was why Marcia loved her cruise pals—they could all just be themselves.

Luscious and Jem used their well-honed skills to procure four bar stools from some accommodating gentlemen. Once ensconced on the bar stools, the women ordered glasses of free rum punch with a Painkiller on the side. Marcia got teased because she unwittingly charmed the bartender into giving her one-and-one-half drinks from his blender, versus the one drink her friends received. Marcia always underestimated her ability to flirt—she was way too sheltered back in WI.

The beach setting was indescribable—everything the women had read about and more. Marcia wished she had packed her palette and paints so she could try to capture all the different blues and greens of the water. If possible, the pristine beach made Marcia feel even more removed from reality than the cruise ship. "Escape" did not do it justice. There were people playing volleyball in the sand, kayaking in the water, laughing at the bar, walking along the beach, dancing to the local-flavor music. Marcia had the choice of being an active participant or a passive one. Marcia chose to be low-key and just people-watch while laughing and drinking with her pals. People-watching was one of Marcia's favorite things to do, especially if she had pals who could help her make up stories about some of the people they saw.

Later, Marcia took a walk alone along the beach, a favorite pastime of hers. Marcia's pals razzed her because Marcia did not just stroll merrily along the waterline. Marcia walked with a roving eye along the beach, looking for shells and coral and driftwood that had special meaning for her. This seemed peculiar to Marcia's pals...why would anyone spend their "Doused Day" free time in this manner? It turned out to be a good beach-combing day. Marcia's search netted a total of four good luck charms—two heart shaped pieces of coral, one heart-shaped stone and one tube-shaped piece of coral. She decided to string one of the coral hearts on a black cord and wear it around her neck for "good mojo." To Marcia, finding these tokens could only mean one thing - L-O-V-E was in the air! Marcia always attached special significance to her beach "finds." Marcia's pals, however, laughed when she described her "treasures." To them, they were just ordinary pieces of coral and rock. It was all a matter of perception.

Marcia's earlier fear of the "Cayamo Cay-gals" consuming mass quantities of rum punch at the "Doused Dollar" and then getting arrested for public intoxication while parasailing was totally unfounded. NO ONE got arrested at the "Doused." A guest could get as soused at the "Doused" as they wished without consequence. No one cared if they had a headache the next day–some guests would simply stay up all night to postpone their headache for a day or two. No one was ready to give up the tranquility of the island and return to the ship late that afternoon. Most guests had, in fact, lost track of reality completely. But more fun awaited them on the ship that night in the form of endless live music.

A long, hot shower in her solo cabin was Marcia's method of reviving herself for the evening ahead. It always felt so good to rinse the remnants of sand and sunscreen and soak her entire body in moisturizer. Once she had dressed in leggings and her favorite polka dot sweater, Marcia had left the beach far behind. She was now in the perfect mood to relax in the amphitheatre with her gal pals. The intimacy of the small theatre allowed Marcia to immerse herself in the magic of the sound. The talented musicians never failed to inspire Marcia. One of her favorite things about cruise ship concerts was the spontaneity of each show and how humble the rock stars came across to their audiences. They acted as though they were just another guest on the music cruise. That night, Marcia and her pals were treated to not only one band on stage but multiple bands simultaneously blending their unique voices and instruments together. Instead of a few musicians on stage, there were musicians filling the entire length of the stage. It was a one-of-a-kind musical experience. Marcia loved to sneak looks at her pals during moments such as these. When she saw the same joyful reaction on their faces, Marcia knew that they, too, felt a strong connection with everyone in the amphitheatre.

Afterwards, the ship's halls buzzed with excited concert review chatter. Although Marcia and her pals were exhausted from the "Doused Dollar", they needed more time to wind down from such an eventful day. The women casually meandered from venue to venue, looking for good "nightcap" music. Marcia felt uncharacteristically subdued and realized it was because she was in such a perfect state of mind. Marcia was filled up with music. There was no better way to transition to a peaceful night's sleep on the ship.

MARCH 17–WEDNESDAY
DAYS ON MUSIC CRUISE=3
DAYS SINCE PROMISE OF CALL FROM IRISH=UNKNOWN–
MARCIA HAD LOST COUNT AND THERE WAS NO PHONE
SERVICE ON SHIP
DAYS SINCE FRIEND REQUEST SENT TO RODNEY=UNKNOWN.
MARCIA HAD LOST COUNT AND HER SELF-IMPOSED SHIP
RULE WAS NO CHECKING E-MAIL OR FACESPACE.COM
**MARCIA'S BEVVIE-OF-THE-MOMENT=STRONG ITALIAN
ROAST WITH 1/2 & 1/2, FROSTY MARGARITAS**
BRANDI'S LYRICS (VIA HEADPHONES) THAT GET HER
THRU=I'M HAPPY CAN'T YOU SEE, I'M ALRIGHT

Marcia spent a large portion of the next day in the ship's casino. She had not planned it that way. Marcia generally stopped into the casino to check out the evening's concert schedule and to sip an afternoon "pick-me-up" cup of coffee. This year, the casino bar was offering a new Italian roast, which was quite tasty. Marcia's favorite bartender, Ozzie, was working that day and had immediately recognized her from the previous year. Ozzie took time out of his busy day to give Marcia a bear hug. Marcia felt VERY special to have Ozzie as a pal–even he if was employed by the cruise line. Ozzie liked Marcia because she was cute and did not over-imbibe (aka get so "schnibbied" that she passed out in the hallway outside of her cabin). Ozzie always paid special attention to Marcia and her bevvie needs.

Marcia finished her Italian roast and meandered slowly though the casino. She had already come to the realization a few nights earlier that she was not a "natural" at the roulette table. The roulette table had been a whole new experience for Marcia. It had been quite entertaining to cheer on a fellow table-mate as he repeatedly picked the correct numbers on the wheel, allowing for his stack of poker chips to grow significantly. Marcia and her cruise pals, however, had not been as lucky. Each of them had lost $20.00 in five minutes flat on the roulette table. The fact that all the casino employees had enthusiastically clapped for them as their dollars got whisked away had not helped their luck at the wheel one bit. Playing Roulette at 3:00 A.M. after an action packed sun, rum-punch and concert-filled day was not, Marcia had realized, a good way to relax.

Today, while her pals gave the Roulette table another try, Marcia decided to play "crack quarters." The name had been coined by another cruise guest and described the game perfectly—once you started playing crack quarters, you simply could not stop. Marcia was attracted to crack quarters because, unlike roulette, they were completely mindless. The concept was simple—quarters that Marcia strategically dropped in pushed other quarters over the edge to the winner's bin—if she was lucky. All that was required was for her to time the quarters so that they fell in the most advantageous way. Crack quarters were an extremely slooooow game, perfectly suited for Marcia.

That evening, Marcia was able to "stay alive" for approximately four hours on ten dollars at a crack quarter machine near the entrance to the casino. At least she thought it was four hours. She really had no clue how long she had been there—and she did not care—Marcia was on vacation. Marcia was known to get a bit carried away at crack quarters. She had, in fact, acquired a reputation among her fellow crack quarter players as "the Crack Quarter Queen." This was probably because Marcia had now been spotted not one, but two years running, at the same crack quarter machine. Marcia was not sure if she should feel honored or not by her newest "title." Either way, she had definitely become a member of what was loosely termed the "Crack Quarter Club." It was a very fun way to meet other cruise guests. They all cheered each other on and applauded each other when one of the machines had a big quarter drop aka "hit." A big "hit" on a crack quarter machine was very loud and exciting for all to hear.

Marcia always played crack quarters in hopes of getting a pink poker chip to drop into her winner's bin. If this occurred, she was rewarded with a bottle of pink champagne, decorated with a pink ribbon. Marcia was attempting to control her on-board liquor bill by winning champagne from the crack quarter machine. The alternative was to purchase a bottle of champagne at the bar for $34.00. Marcia's pink poker chip strategy was not without flaws – her latest bottle of champagne had cost her MORE than $34.00! Marcia felt like this was a small price to pay for the entertainment it provided her, as well as the other cruise guests who stopped to watch the crack quarter players.

Currently, a pink poker chip was nowhere near the edge and the casino band had started to play. Marcia decided it was time for a break from crack quarters. Her cruise pals were nowhere to be found. The roulette table and/ or strong drinks may have done them in for the night.

Marcia was not yet done in for the night. She had kept her wits about her by drinking Pepsi at the crack quarter machine. Marcia was buzzed on only sugar. Before long, she found herself dancing ALONE on the casino dance floor. She could not resist. The band had started to play Pure Prairie League's "Amy"—a song that Marcia had always loved. It was so freaking fun to dance alone—Marcia did not give a rip what people thought of her. She felt as free as a bird—so free that she continued to dance to the next song, a combination of "Mystic" and "Free." Marcia was not familiar with "Free" but decided that it was one of the coolest tunes she had yet heard on the cruise.

She was joined on the dance floor by her newest pal, Anne "with an E" and another female cruise guest whom she had not yet met. There was no need for introductions - the three of them totally rocked the dance floor until it became packed with other cruisers. Later, another rock star took to the stage for a jam session with the casino band and performed "Crazy", another song dear to Marcia's heart. Marcia had SO MUCH FUN DANCING! HER LEGS WOULD BE ABSOLUTELY KILLING HER THE NEXT DAY BUT IT WAS SO WORTH IT! Marcia could not remember the last time she had danced non-stop. The feeling she experienced was just like when she had dunked her head in the ocean. Marcia had somehow forgotten how much she loved to dance.

It was 4:00 A.M when Marcia finally inserted her key card into her cabin door. Her arms were filled with bottles of pink champagne. Marcia smiled and wondered if any of her gal pals had missed her that evening. Between dancing up a storm in the casino and then playing more crack quarters with the band's security crew, Marcia had totally lost track of time. She had plenty of stories with which to entertain her pals the next day. Only Marcia would be bold enough to hang out with the band's security guards, who had stopped in to the casino after a long work night. Although some of the crew looked tough, they were SO sweet to Marcia, and went the extra mile to make sure Marcia felt "protected", out alone at 3:00 A.M. Marcia was impressed that these men would go out of their way for her, especially after such a busy night of concerts. Marcia also loved their sense of humor. After she explained her "pink poker chip" crack quarter strategy to the crew, they were so generous that they donated all of their champagne winnings to Marcia. Marcia was very touched by this gesture. When she finally said goodnight to the crew members, they were perfect gentlemen and assured Marcia that they would keep an eye out for her at upcoming shows. All in all, it had been another perfect evening on the ship.

MARCH 18–THURSDAY
DAYS ON MUSIC CRUISE=4
DAYS SINCE PROMISE OF CALL FROM IRISH=UNKNOWN–
MARCIA HAD LOST COUNT AND THERE WAS NO PHONE
SERVICE ON SHIP
DAYS SINCE FRIEND REQUEST SENT TO RODNEY=UNKNOWN.
MARCIA HAD LOST COUNT AND HER SELF-IMPOSED SHIP
RULE WAS NO CHECKING E-MAIL OR FACESPACE.COM
**MARCIA'S BEVVIE-OF-THE-MOMENT = FRESH MANGO
DAIQUIRIS**
BRANDI'S LYRICS (VIA HEADPHONES) THAT GET HER
THRU=I'M HAPPY CAN'T YOU SEE, I'M ALRIGHT

Day four of the cruise–another port of call–offered guests several entertainment options away from the ship. The ship was currently docked at yet another island which, terrain-wise, was remarkably different from the "Doused Dollar" island. Marsha chose to spend the day with some new cruise pals from Colorado who were privy to an all-inclusive package at one of the private beaches. There were a limited number of guest slots along this private coast. As soon as their ramshackle bus pulled up to expanse of beautiful white sand surrounded by pseudo-jungle greenery, Marcia knew she had made the right decision. Most of the other cruise guests had been dropped off earlier at the "townie" beach. The "townie" beach, even though above-average by beach standards, was bustling with activity. Marcia was more in the mood for an escape from the crowds on the ship and felt fortunate to have been offered such a tranquil alternative.

Today's definition of "all-inclusive" translated to:

- All-you-could-drink frozen rum daiquiris, served beachside by cute, flirty, attentive bartenders. The daiquiris came in a variety of fresh-fruit flavors and were so smooth they could be sucked down with a straw in a matter of minutes. Marcia alternated between fresh mango (her favorite thus far), and banana (a close second). She still planned on sampling several other flavors before the sun set that day.

- FREE bottled spring water. Bottled spring water was a port of call–and cruise ship–commodity. Bottled spring water was

NEVER free. Bottled water fell into a category all its own. It was extremely important to stay hydrated in such a warm climate. Cruise guests would pay any price for a bottle of fresh water so getting free bottled water was a real treat.

- FREE chaise lounges. Chaise lounge availability worked a lot like spring water availability. There were very few beaches that provided chaise lounges gratis. To kick back on a FREE chaise lounge while drinking FREE daiquiris AND FREE bottled spring water was a heavenly experience.

There were also FREE nachos to help offset the mass quantities of daiquiris consumed on the beach. Granted, nachos were not quite as fancy of a lunch as, say, surf and turf. However, at least Marcia was able to identify all of the ingredients in the nachos she had seen being served on the beach. Marcia was feeling a bit traumatized by the "FISH GUTTING FRENZY" she had been witness to earlier that day. She had noticed a group of local fishermen carrying a humongous grouper to the pristine shoreline. The fish was so big it took three men to transport—and they were struggling under its weight. The fishermen extracted a large slab of wood from one of two boats docked nearby. They set the slab under an old deadwood tree that for some reason stuck right out of the shoreline. First, the men unceremoniously chopped the head off of the fish. Marcia cringed at the sight of this but felt compelled to keep watching. As if this weren't disturbing enough, the men then proceeded to calmly slice open the fish belly and de-gut the fish. The fishermen were totally oblivious to the horrified sunbathers sitting on the beach behind them. Marcia never knew a fish could have so many guts. At this point, all Marcia hoped was that her mango daiquiris would stay settled in her stomach. She was feeling more than a bit queasy.

By now, there was a small group of men surrounding the local fishermen, eager to get involved in the fish-gutting process. All Marcia could think was that a fish-gutting of this magnitude signified a special "male bonding" ritual that women would be hard-pressed to understand.

After burying the fish guts in the sand, the fishermen then set off with the "cutting board" across the beach to the lone restaurant. Marcia, being her usual paranoid self, imagined the be-headed, de-gutted, sun-warmed, maggot-filled monstrosity magically transformed into the restaurants fish taco "Special of the Day." She could just picture the men behind the restaurant, chopping up the enormous fish into bite-sized pieces and handing them off to the chef. It was now very close to lunchtime. FREE Nachos were sounding better all the time.

RANDOM THOUGHT: Marcia was one of the few people on the beach who would actually spend time contemplating why the fishermen's boats were named Lissie I and Lissie II. Why was there a Lissie I AND a Lissie II? Was Lissie the name of one of their daughters? The name of one of their wives? Was Lissie I such a lucky fishing vessel that her name was carried over for use on Lissie II? Marcia would probably never discover the reasoning behind the duplicated name. She came to the conclusion that Lissie must have been an extra-special relative who warranted honor on not one but two separate fishing boats.

After lunch, Marcia decided to take a stroll along the beach boardwalk to check out the local vendors wares. Marcia's well-trained eyes immediately spotted a sign on the boardwalk that read "MASSAGES." An arrow on the sign pointed to a second floor balcony attached to the restaurant. Without hesitation, Marcia climbed the stairs to the balcony. She knew this was an opportunity worth checking out. Island massages were few and far between. If the low-key local people she had met that day were any indication, Marcia would be wise to investigate further. The cost of a massage, Marcia justified, would be easily offset by the free daiquiris.

Fifteen minutes later, Marcia found herself face down on a massage table, being caressed by strong hands and the warm ocean breeze. Marcia had one fleeting moment of self consciousness when she realized her winter-white butt was on display to everyone on the beach. Not to mention her breasts. "Who cares," Marcia thought, "this is all part of island life." No one here gave a second thought to milky-white butts or breasts. She could easily get accustomed to sprawling butt-naked on gorgeous beaches such as this one. It was the perfect way to spend a lazy afternoon. Instead of baking in the intense sun, Marcia was now relaxing in the shade, while simultaneously prepping herself for more all-night dancing on the ship. The "open-air" massage turned out to be one of the best Marcia had ever experienced.

Marcia returned to her chaise lounge in a Gumby-like state. She had time for one last mango daiquiri before the beach day came to an end. Marcia and her pal Anne spent the next several minutes laughing while discussing the merits of the lone male strolling down the beach in a mankini. The sight was distracting in an unusual sort of way. Marcia had never seen a man in a mankini before and tried not to stare rudely at the construction of the swimsuit. Marcia and Anne quickly came to the conclusion that it took an extraordinary man to pull off a mankini. Unfortunately, their "mankini specimen" of the day did not fall into the "extraordinary" category.

Marcia wished she could stay longer at the gorgeous beach, doing nothing more than sipping daiquiris and eying mankini-clad men. It was hard to believe that this was the last port of call on the cruise. At least she had more music and dancing and laughter to look forward to on the ship that night. Marcia planned on savoring every minute of it.

Being back on board the ship that evening proved to be a stark contrast to Marcia's peaceful island day trip. Not long after the ship set sail, the weather took a nasty turn. The waves off of the seventh deck were unlike any Marcia had ever seen. Roiling, powerful, grey-black masses that rocked the ship in an alarming fashion. Marcia overheard another guest say the waves were fifteen feet high. Marcia thought that might be a conservative estimate. Marcia's stomach was feeling a little "FISH GUTTING FRENZY-ISH" but she was one of the luckier guests. Marcia was still able to navigate around the ship, even if it meant bouncing from one side of the hall to the other. Roughly one-third of the other cruise guests were, unfortunately, spending their night lying on their cabin bunks, warding off seasickness. Dramamine patches had become a black market item of sorts, selling for record prices. Marcia would probably have every dance floor on the ship entirely to herself, as long as the bands were able to maintain their balance on the stage.

For the first time, Marcia was glad that her cabin had a lifeboat located right outside her porthole. Marcia had wasted the entire cruise safety drill in her cabin, searching frantically for the life jacket that the crew assured her they had supplied. Not only was there no life jacket in Marcia's cabin, she had no clue where to assemble should there be an actual emergency. No matter—Marcia was one step ahead of the emergency plan. All she had to do was climb through her cabin porthole in order to secure a place in the lifeboat. Surely lifeboats were equipped with life jackets–it only made sense. Once Marcia actually got INTO the lifeboat, she could figure out how to actually detach the lifeboat from the ship wall. Marcia felt confident that she would make an excellent life boat captain in a pinch. Still, she hoped she would not be called upon to do so later that evening.

While roaming the ship halls, contemplating what to do next, Marcia encountered a uniformed crew member. He informed her that she would need to return to her cabin and shut the porthole, due to the rough seas. This was a bit alarming since Marcia was on the EIGHTH deck. Marcia immediately went to her cabin and attempted to "follow orders" but quickly realized she did not have the strength to pull the porthole door shut. Let alone tighten the porthole wheel. Marcia did not feel comfortable with the "batten down the hatches" order anyway. She felt it was important to keep her own emergency plan in place. A little seawater in her bed would be tolerable.

By now, feeling frustrated and drenched in sweat, Marcia decided it would be the perfect time to find her "little brown jug." Her "little brown jug" aka her emergency cabin booze was conveniently filled with spiced rum. Marcia had purchased it at her favorite port-of-call spice shop, along with the special Hurricane Hot Peppa Sauce (Levels 1, 2, 3 and 4) packaged in tiny bottles and decorated with tiny straw hats. Her "little brown jug" came in a small glass bottle accented with cross-hatched banana fronds. Marcia had been excited to see it sported an even bigger straw hat. Marcia believed that these miniature straw hats were one of the coolest inventions in the Caribbean. They also made the best souvenirs.

At this point on the cruise, Marcia was too broke to purchase any type of mixer, such as orange juice or coke, for her spiced rum. Marcia's on-board cruise tab currently reflected a $1,333 balance, even though she had snuck tequila on the ship. She now had no choice but to mix her spiced rum with free beverages from the buffet–either glasses of water or iced tea. Tonight, she decided that her best course of action was to simply guzzle the rum directly from the jug. Marcia felt more stressed than she had since leaving Haystack. The stormy weather had not been conducive to a relaxing night on the ship. Marcia knew the rum would help take the edge off.

Later, while out on the smoking deck observing the still-rolling seas, Marcia heard that another male passenger had been discovered lying naked in bed when the order to "batten down the hatches" came in. The man was passed out after too many shots of tequila. In order to close the porthole in his cabin, a female crew member had to climb over him on his bed. Marcia felt relieved that she had managed to keep her spiced rum consumption under control that evening. She would have been mortified had she been found unconscious, naked, snoring in her bed by a crew member. Marcia had no desire to acquire a reputation as a "schnibbied" cruise guest. She was, in fact, feeling a bit tipsy from the spiced rum combined with the ship's motion and decided it would be best if she turned in for the night. The following day was her last full day of vacation and Marcia did not want to spend it with a large hangover.

MARCH 19–FRIDAY
DAYS ON MUSIC CRUISE=5
DAYS SINCE PROMISE OF CALL FROM IRISH=UNKNOWN–
MARCIA HAD LOST COUNT AND THERE WAS NO PHONE
SERVICE ON SHIP
DAYS SINCE FRIEND REQUEST SENT TO RODNEY=UNKNOWN.
MARCIA HAD LOST COUNT AND HER SELF-IMPOSED SHIP
RULE WAS NO CHECKING E-MAIL OR FACESPACE.COM
**MARCIA'S BEVVIE-OF-THE-MOMENT=GOURMET CRUISE
SHIP CAPPUCCINO**
BRANDI'S LYRICS (VIA HEADPHONES) THAT GET HER
THRU=I'M HAPPY CAN'T YOU SEE, I'M ALRIGHT

The next morning Marcia was out on the seventh deck of the ship, smoking furiously. She was reeling after having just met a handsome man named Gustav from Darmstadt, Germany. Earlier, Marcia had splurged on her first and only "gourmet" cup of coffee for the day, in order to prepare for a carefree morning spent writing on the seventh deck. Marcia had desperately felt the need to record the events of the past few days on the music cruise. They would all too quickly be replaced with events from the current day. Marcia had been sipping her cappuccino while appreciating the beautiful sight of the sun just beginning to peek through the dissipating storm clouds. The seventh deck provided an amazing open-air view. Marcia could actually lean over the side of the enormous ship and gaze out at the vast expanse of the ocean. It was mesmerizing. The waves–still strong from the stormy weather–foamed up and back again into the mass of water.

Marcia was simply minding her own business at 6:45 on a gorgeous Friday morning. It was technically the last day of the music and the cruise, for all practical purposes. The ship would dock in Miami at 8:00 A.M. the following morning. There was only one more night of concerts to look forward to. It was bittersweet–vacation had flown by very quickly.

Marcia would generally run into other people while out on the seventh deck; it was a popular spot to smoke. She felt guilty about sneaking a cigarette with her cappuccino while the "walking club" stormed past her. The walkers were no doubt irked that they had to walk through a cloud of smoke while getting their daily exercise. Marcia was trying not to feel bad about this–she was on vacation, after all–when the deck door suddenly opened and an extremely attractive man stepped out, holding an unlit cigarette (no coffee, Marcia noted). Marcia felt her pulse race a bit and inwardly tried to slow it down.

Marcia and the attractive man had casually started chatting and continued chatting over the course of three cigarettes (attractive man); 1 cigarette (Marcia). Introductions were made on a first-name basis. Gustav was forty-seven years old, super cute, and had a great accent. As they talked, Marcia's wild imagination immediately kicked in, even though she had none of the pertinent "facts" about Gustav. Facts such as: his last name, his marital status and most importantly, his telephone number. Marcia knew a telephone number was a bit premature but Marcia was known for her ability to move fast. Gustav had been so down to earth and friendly. Marcia HAD found out two pertinent snippets of information:

1. Gustav was on the cruise with "a friend." Marcia was fairly certain that this "friend" was female. But because the conversation with Gustav was so easy, Marcia had decided not to let that info deter her.

2. Gustav was staying on the tenth deck of the ship. This was not much to go on, given the number of cabins on each floor. But it was something and Marcia was nothing, if not resourceful.

Now Marcia was plotting and writing simultaneously, while savoring her last hours in a swimsuit. She decided she would get super-gussied-up that night, with the hope of running into Gustav again at the 8:00 concert. Marcia knew they were scheduled for the same show. There were only 900 people to identify in the theatre–Marcia felt she had a good chance of finding Gustav. Marcia had also mentioned to Gustav what a fun venue the casino was–how rock stars would randomly show up "after hours" and jam with the casino band. If she did not see Gustav at the main concert, Marcia reasoned, perhaps he would head over to the casino later in the evening. Truthfully, Gustav did NOT seem like the type that hung out in a casino. Although Marcia really did not seem like that type either. But anything was possible.

Sub-consciously, Marcia was hoping to replicate the whirlwind romance that was brewing between one of her new cruise pals and an East Coast

DEA agent. Her pal had met the DEA agent while enjoying a cocktail in a hotel lounge the night before the cruise began. Ironically, the DEA agent currently had a pending case in Idaho, which was where her new pal resided. There was real potential for the DEA agent to plan a "social visit" to Idaho. Marcia was very happy for her new friend. After all, wasn't this what single people were looking for - a romance triggered by a chance meeting in a hotel lounge? Or a chance meeting on a music cruise?

It suddenly dawned on Marcia that opportunities like the "hotel lounge romance" never happened to her. In fact, Marcia sometimes struggled when she heard stories of recent divorcees IMMEDIATELY finding what they hoped was the "real thing." Marcia had been looking for the "real thing" for fifteen years! Marcia sometimes felt she would be looking for the rest of her life! Marcia sometimes felt like she would always be alone and NEVER FIND "THE FREAKING ONE" aka BOY-FOR-ALL-SEASONS, while everyone else effortlessly rolled into "the real thing" with "the real one." Marcia knew she had to keep a positive attitude but it was very hard. Especially when the first impression Marcia generally made during a chance meeting with a man was that she was a "psycho woman."

Now Marcia was beating herself up because SHE was the one who had ended the conversation with Gustav that morning. She was the one who had nipped her one freaking chance encounter in the bud. Gustav had seemed in no hurry to leave the ship deck. Marcia was the one who had to open her big mouth and tell Gustav, of all things, that he'd better go take his medication! CRAP, WHY DID MARCIA ALWAYS DO STUFF LIKE THAT? It must have been nerves. She could have, at least, let Gustav be the one to end their conversation! She could have, at least, asked for his business card and/or last name and/or any info that would allow her to follow up with Gustav. Marcia should have thought up an excuse–ANY excuse–in order to get Gustav's personal info. She was usually so good at making up stories on the fly. As a last resort, Marcia should have simply whipped out her Whisks R Us business card and presented it to Gustav.

Marcia was extremely disappointed that she had not gotten Gustav's business card, but geez, what did she expect from a three-cigarette conversation? Especially when she did most of the talking? Marcia needed to keep her "hopeless romantic" self in check but that seemed impossible for her to do. The thought of a long-distance romance with a German man was so exciting compared to the thought of the cold, harsh reality Marcia had to return to in a mere twenty-four hours.

In Marcia's eyes, she and Gustav were simply a match made in heaven. Marcia's ability to envision romantic potential was exactly what set her apart from other women, what made her so special. Marcia's ability to turn the few simple bits of information that she and Gustav shared (Daughters who were obsessed with the band Tokio Hotel, the fact that they both had to take medication every morning, and how they both loved to see the sun rise over the ocean) into a full-fledged love affair was the very reason that Marcia would one day find true love! It all made sense to her now. Marcia never gave up! Ultimately, it did not matter if, in the process, Marcia created heartache for herself. The fact that she could IMAGINE a love affair, IMAGINE the possibilities, was something she would never change.

Gustav fit nicely into Marcia's realm of possibility. Neither Gustav nor Marcia had much time but Marcia, being the daughter of a CPA, did have good business sense. Surely Gustav must travel to the U.S. on a regular basis, Marcia reasoned. Using her Whisks R Us contacts, Marcia could help Gustav develop potential new customers all over the U.S. It followed that Gustav would then have reason to come to Wisconsin on business - just like the DEA agent from the East Coast! Marcia could pick Gustav up at the MSP airport while she was in the Twin Cities picking up scalp whisks! Gustav would not only be blown away by Marcia's savvy business "know-how", he would be love-struck by her charm and wit and uniqueness. Gustav would constantly be jumping on red-eye flights to wine and dine Marcia. They would have sleepovers in posh downtown Minneapolis hotels! Gustav could even come and visit Marcia in Haystack!

How cool would it be if Marcia ended up meeting the man of her dreams, her BOY-FOR-THE-WINTER (or even her BOY-FOR-ALL-SEASONS) on the very LAST day of the music cruise! A man who, incidentally, happened to reside in a foreign country! Forget the East Coast DEA agent! Marcia was not only known as a dreamer, she was known for dreaming BIG! It would be somewhat fitting for her to go for the freaking gusto and track down Gustav and end up living large by dating a man who was 4,000 miles away! It would be perrrrrfect!

Marcia still had 1 hour and 2 minutes to record thoughts on her laptop before her battery died. Marcia would use this time to simply add her imaginary Gustav long-distance love affair story to her novel-in-progress. Realistically, Gustav was probably traveling with a beautiful European woman. Men with Gustav's looks and charm generally did not travel alone. In reality, Marcia's actual chances of romance were slim. But Marcia WAS a dreamer and so she decided to do what she did at yoga class—offer up an "intention" for the day. Marcia silently breathed her intention—to get a second "chance encounter" with Gustav—to herself.

Marcia highly doubted that she had made a stellar first impression on Gustav earlier that morning. How was she to know that she would be meeting a cute German on the seventh deck? Upon awakening, she had simply thrown on her baggy brown shorts and green hoodie. Flew out of her cabin with bed-head hair, swollen eyes, and un-brushed teeth breath (but they had been smoking anyway, right?) in order to catch the sunrise on the water. Her only saving grace, appearance-wise, had been the 2009 Cayamo T-shirt she had been wearing. It was at least a bit more fitted than her XL Gaelic Storm T-shirt—in other words, Gustav would have been able to take note of her shapely upper bod (riiiiight). Marcia would need to keep the seventh deck on her radar today. It was one of the few places on the humongous ship where a person COULD smoke, so the chances of running into Gustav there were higher than, say, the buffet line.

By now, Marcia was feeling a little depressed. She always felt this way after constructing an imaginary love story in her head. She vowed to open the damn bottle of "crack quarter" pink champagne tonight and get schnibbied before the 8:00 concert. Champagne would help relax Marcia so she could toddle in to the concert. The ship's natural rocking motion would cover up the fact that she was, indeed, tipsy.

Suddenly, Marcia had a brilliant idea. Forget the pink champagne. She would need her ENTIRE BOTTLE OF FREAKING SOUVENIER ST. CROIX TEQUILA to bolster her courage enough to pull off such a crazy idea. She would also need to enlist the help of the "Cayamo Cay-gals." Her idea was simple: if all else failed in the "Hunt for Gustav", the women could convene on the tenth deck while guests were attending concerts that evening. The ship had provided cute "message boards" on each cabin door. The message boards had a space for "NAME", "WHERE ARE YOU

FROM?" and "ALUMNI STATUS", along with "FAVORITE MOMENT SO FAR." Marcia and her pals could read every freaking message board on the tenth deck, in hopes of finding Gustav's cabin. If they were successful, Marcia could add a cryptic message (aka her name and phone number) to Gustav's message board. Gustav had seemed like the kind of detail-oriented guy who would take the time to read his message board.

Ironically, Marcia had returned to her cabin only the night before to find the words "Cindy here—no Robert or John" scribbled on HER message board. Marcia had pondered what this message could mean for several minutes before writing it off to an impulsive drunken guest. Marcia could only hope that Gustav would not do the same—that Gustav would take her message seriously.

Marcia decided she had absolutely nothing to lose by acting like a wild and crazy "psycho-woman" on her last night of the cruise. Marcia hated missed opportunities. This was just like a rock star "autograph op"–it was best to be prepared just in case. Marcia was on a Gustav MISSION!

Marcia suddenly wished she could get feedback from Betty, back home in Wisconsin. Betty would certainly be proud of Marcia for deviating from her usual $42.99 per bottle Patron Silver tequila habit and purchasing a $26 bottle of St. Croix Agave tequila instead. Marcia could picture Betty right now, downing a shot of the St. Croix Agave tequila with her, while advising Marcia on how to proceed with tracking down Gustav. Marcia was pretty sure Betty would approve whole-heartedly of the tequila-fueled message board plan. Betty would tell Marcia to GO FOR IT! Even if it meant that Betty would have to forgo sharing any SOUVENIR Agave tequila with Marcia.

Oddly, Marcia had not seen ANY of the "Cayamo Cay-gals" that day, although meeting Gustav had distracted her from all other thoughts. Besides, Marcia wanted to savor her few bittersweet moments alone with Gustav. Marcia had earlier vowed to herself that she would NOT tell ANYONE about Gustav. Marcia had been blabbing WAY TOO FREAKING MUCH on the boat. It came with the territory. However, with the advent of her latest hair-brain "message board scheme", she now had to tell the "Cayamo Cay-gals" everything. It was unavoidable. Now was the time to enlist their help, which Marcia desperately needed. It was now or never.

A few hours later, Marcia had switched into high gear. The theme for the last night on the ship was "Black Tie." Marcia was now freshly showered, shaved and shorn. Her bed-head hair was teased to the hilt. She had gone totally out of her comfort zone and donned her grape-purple slinky velvet cocktail dress. It was the sexiest dress Marcia had ever purchased. She was even wearing silver high-heeled sandals that looked like something from a Disney Princess book. She left a trail of perfume all the way down the cabin hallway, en route to the seventh deck for a "Gustav check" before the 8:00 concert. Marcia had even remembered to spray perfume on the back of her knees. She had also tipped back a large courage shot of Agave tequila–Marcia was susceptible to blushing when wearing dresses that left little to the imagination. No detail had been overlooked in her personal appearance. Marcia hoped the "Cayamo Cay-gals" had also dressed up so she would not feel too out of place.

Marcia's attention to detail was already paying off. She had received appreciative looks from a group of younger men who had accompanied her in the elevator to the seventh deck. One of the men had even told her that she looked amazing in her purple gown. Marcia was now trying to compose herself–the man had been no more than 25 years old! Marcia was feeling a bit flushed and decided the best course of action was a margarita.

Once she had armed herself with a margarita, Marcia retreated to the relative calm of the seventh deck. This, in itself, was a bit of a challenge. Marcia had scored a first from the ship bartender–a bonus SIDE margarita, at no additional charge. Marcia assumed the bartender's benevolence had been due to her slinky dress, as well as her winning smile. The only drawback to clutching a margarita in each hand was now figuring out how to actually open the door to the ship deck.

Surprisingly, she was completely alone on the seventh deck. There was no sign of Gustav. The tequila was helping Marcia to relax – instead of feeling upset, she was having silly, random thoughts like the realization that her ears were sunburned. She suddenly remembered having a conversation with a fellow cruise mate who took his wife to the upper-most deck of the ship in the middle of the storm. The man wanted to recreate the "Titanic" experience for his wife simply because his wife loved standing in the wind. Marcia took a moment now to peer over the deck rail, imagining what it would be like to have such a loving, creative partner. A partner that was considerate enough to re-enact a romantic, cinematic moment at sea.

Suddenly, a big gust of wind slammed Marcia on the side of her head. The blast was strong enough to dislodge her eyeglass stems from behind her sunburned ears. Marcia watched in horror as her glasses flew off her face and fell down, down, down into the dark ocean waters below. "NOOOOOOOOO," screamed Marcia. In her tequila-altered state, it took a few moments for Marcia to fully comprehend what had just happened. Her first sickening thought was that she had now messed up ANY chance of finding Gustav at the concert that night. Marcia was COMPLETELY blind without her glasses. She would no longer be able to differentiate between Gustav and, say, the sound engineer, at the concert. Especially on Black Tux night.

Marcia needed to regroup–the concert was starting in ten minutes. There was no way to recover her glasses–they were gone forever. Marcia had a fleeting moment of guilt about the fact that she had littered in the ocean. Get a grip, she told herself. There was no way to rectify the situation. Marcia now had to race to her cabin in a tizzy and find her only "back-up"–her large, dark prescription sunglasses! Now, not only would Marcia be sight AND light-impaired at the concert, she would feel mortified that her slinky image was marred by her dorky prescription sunglasses! Marcia's big-haired confidence was rapidly diminishing. But her sunglasses were her only hope.

Once Marcia had donned her sunglasses, the night went swiftly downhill. The concert was a bust. Marcia was not able to see any of the musicians, let alone find Gustav, in the amphitheatre. She had made the best of it by removing her dorky sunglasses and simply closing her eyes and taking in the beautiful sound of the music. She was grateful that her backup plan–the "Gustav message board scheme" –was already in place. Marcia, for once, did not have to THINK AHEAD.

After the concert, Marcia went to the casino in search of the "Cayamo Cay-gals." It was now time to set the wheels of the "Gustav message board scheme" into motion. The cabin halls were quiet and empty; all of the guests were out living it up on their last night of the cruise. Fortunately, Marcia was able to find her gal pals at the roulette table and explain her dilemma. This took a while, especially since Marcia was only semi-coherent. She had exceeded her usual conservative level of tequila, in hopes of boosting her self-confidence. Her pals were skeptical of Marcia's seventh deck tale and questioned whether Marcia had simply contrived Gustav out of thin air. Was Marcia being her usual "Cry Wolf" self? Was there an actual, live man involved or was Marcia fabricating the entire story?

Being the good friends that they were, the "Cay-gals" decided to give Marcia the benefit of the doubt and offered their assistance with the tenth deck message board plan. They complimented Marcia on the ingeniousness of her scheme. All of the women were tipsy enough to go along with it. If nothing else, it would create a silly, lasting memory of their last night together on the ship.

Once the women had taken the elevator to the tenth deck, they quickly split up the cabin numbers between each of them. It would not be hard to locate Gustav's cabin, they reasoned–how many guests named Gustav could be staying on the tenth deck? Marcia had brought black pens and Whisks R Us business cards to distribute to the other three women. She also asked them to remove their sandals, in case they had to flee the premises on short notice. Marcia did not want to be responsible for one of the women breaking their ankle while running in 3-inch heels. Besides, Marcia reasoned, the freedom of bare feet would help them to accomplish their mission. If they were successful, Marcia planned on uncorking the pink champagne in her cabin for a midnight toast. Her pals were all for this idea and agreed to meet back at the elevators in a half-hour.

Marcia began to navigate from cabin to cabin, carefully reviewing the message board on each door. Even though she still felt like a character in a Disney princess story, Marcia was sober enough to appreciate the fact that she was actually taking a real-live chance. Marcia was going after something she wanted versus simply imagining the possibilities. This was a big step for Marcia and she was proud that she was not letting the Gustav "autograph op" pass her by.

Suddenly, Marcia heard a commotion down the hall. She ran in her bare feet to find Luscious Brown, screaming, jumping up and down, and pointing excitedly to cabin 1044. Marcia trained her bleary gaze on the cabin door. There, big as life, next to the message board "NAME" was a neatly printed "GUSTAV." All of the women quickly gathered around the cabin door and thought up witty messages that Marcia could use to relay her personal info to Gustav. Marcia would not listen to any of them – she wanted to keep the message short and sweet. Just her First Name and her Phone Number. Gustav was an intelligent man–he would understand her message and act accordingly. All Marcia could do now was to make her information available on the message board. The rest was up to Gustav.

MARCH 20–SATURDAY
DAYS ON MUSIC CRUISE=6
DAYS SINCE PROMISE OF CALL FROM IRISH=UNKNOWN–
MARCIA HAD LOST COUNT AND THERE WAS NO PHONE
SERVICE ON SHIP
DAYS SINCE FRIEND REQUEST SENT TO RODNEY=UNKNOWN.
MARCIA HAD LOST COUNT AND HER SELF-IMPOSED SHIP
RULE WAS NO CHECKING E-MAIL OR FACESPACE.COM
**MARCIA'S BEVVIE-OF-THE-MOMENT=MARGINAL BUFFET
LINE COFFEE WITH CREAM**
LYRICS (NOT VIA HEADPHONES) THAT GET HER THRU
WHILE SITTING IN THE HOT TUB=UNDETERMINED, SHE
CANNOT MAKE OUT ANY OF THE SHIP "ELEVATOR MUSIC"
SONGS

Marcia was up early the next morning. She had no choice–her suitcase
was packed so full it would not close. Marcia had to figure out what she
could leave behind from her luggage in order to exit the cruise ship and
successfully board an airplane home. Marcia's choices were limited to a
few select items–her buckwheat pillow or the costume she had packed
and worn for "Toga Day" on the cruise. It did not take her long to decide.
Marcia doubted she would have any further use for her toga outfit in
Wisconsin. Her special pillow, however, was something she could not live
without. She ditched the toga outfit, including the artificial ivy she had
used as a "crown", in her cabin wastebasket and finally got all of the zippers
to close on her suitcase.

Marcia still had enough time to go up to the pool deck and take a farewell
soak in the ship's hot tub. By now, she was used to exposing her Wisconsin
cellulite in front of crowds of people. In fact, ever since her "open-air" beach
massage, Marcia had learned to expose her cleavage as well. Marcia had
learned to FREAKING FLAUNT her 50-year-old cleavage! No one on the
cruise ship had seemed to mind. Sure, Marcia's 50-year-old cleavage was
not quite as perky as some of the 20 year-olds onboard but, nonetheless,
Marcia had been blessed in this respect so she had nothing to lose. Before
the cruise, Marcia had felt uncomfortable when men would check out her
curves but she was now feeling more at ease. Both Marcia and her cleavage
were pretty darn cute.

Marcia quickly changed into her swim suit and made her way to the soothing salt water of the hot tub. There were no other cruise guests around—everyone was busy preparing for their departure. It was a beautiful morning in Miami. Marcia was treated to the sight of the sun rising above the ocean. Seeing the sun rise on the water was one of the things Marcia would miss the most when she returned home to the arctic air of Wisconsin. Now, Marcia relaxed in the warm hot tub water and thought about all the other things she would miss as well.

Marcia would miss the distraction that crack quarters provided, but not that much. Marcia would miss the beautiful casino bar, with the different flavored vodka bottles lined up to perfection. Marcia would miss the bartenders breaking out in impromptu dances as they poured drinks. Marcia would miss going out to the smoking deck only to happen upon a "photo op" of a musician playing shuffleboard (the photo would end up being used as his next CD cover). Marcia would miss her cabin towels folded craftily into elephant and other animal shapes with her sunglasses perched on their towel-trunks/noses. Marcia would miss having her bed made. Marcia would miss being up before the crowd so there was no waiting line at the "good" coffee bar. Marcia would miss the sense of accomplishment she felt after boarding the ship with smuggled tequila stashed in her backpack … and not getting pulled out of line and sent to the "naughty room." Not that Marcia ever HAD been sent to the "naughty room" - but only because up until that time she had never risked it. Marcia would miss dark Bass Ale poured into frosted mugs embellished with the cruise line logo. Marcia really wanted one of those mugs as a souvenir. Except Marcia did not know how she would snitch a mug without getting caught and thrown in jail at the Port of Miami. Marcia decided a souvenir mug was not worth getting arrested over.

She interrupted her carefree thoughts to glance up at the clock posted near the hot tub. Below the clock, a sign read "Who cares what time it is, anyway?" Marcia decided that not having to worry about "what time it was" might end up being the thing she would miss most of all. Sadly, it was now time for Marcia to bid farewell to the hot tub and go prepare for her own departure from the ship.

MARCH 21–SUNDAY
DAYS SINCE MUSIC CRUISE=1
DAYS SINCE PROMISE OF CALL FROM IRISH=N/A
MARCIA COULD LIVE WITHOUT RACING COVERALLS.
REPLACED WITH POTENTIAL CALL FROM GUSTAV IN
GERMANY!
DAYS SINCE FRIEND REQUEST SENT TO RODNEY=FELT LIKE
94 DAYS. MARCIA HAD LOST COUNT (SHE DID NOT REALIZE
SHE COULD CALCULATE THE NUMBER BASED ON THE
LENGTH OF THE CRUISE)
**MARCIA'S   BEVVIE-OF-THE-MOMENT=STARBUCKS
STRAWBERRY BANANA SMOOTHIE WITH WHEY PROTEIN
POWDER**
BRANDI'S LYRICS (VIA HEADPHONES) THAT GET HER
THRU=IN A CROWDED ROOM, I'M ALONE

Reality quickly set in at the Chicago airport. Marcia was NOT having a good day. Marcia had been stranded at the airport for the last thirty-six hours due to a monster blizzard in Minneapolis. A whopping 27" of snow had already fallen, with additional snow predicted.

The airport was a zoo. Total chaos, unlike Marcia had ever seen before. Passengers had literally been at the airport for two days, with little hope of getting home that afternoon. Marcia had recently joined the throng of "not getting home" people. She was currently number 65 on Stand-by for the next connection to Minneapolis–Flight 444. There were a total of 89 people currently on Stand-by for Flight 444.

Marcia had rushed, literally ran, to the connecting flight gate to try to make her flight, only to find out there was no freaking reason to rush - Stand-by passenger number 65 was not going ANYWHERE soon. Marcia did not understand how she had made the transition from a paid-in-full passenger on Flight 444 to number 65 on Stand-By. But nothing was making sense at the Chicago airport that day. Nothing was making sense at ANY major airport that day–the entire nation had been affected by the record snowstorm.

Everyone at the gate was extremely grumpy, harried, even snapping at one another. Marcia had not minded one whit traveling solo that day. Who needed snappish traveling companions anyway? In fact, Marcia was single-handedly the luckiest passenger at the gate—she had been the ONLY one to get stranded in MIAMI the previous night. Granted, her luggage had gone on to La Guardia in New York (a SUPER logical destination, in Marcia's eyes). It was the ONLY time Marcia had not been prepared for such an event by carrying on a backpack filled with lost luggage essentials. Marcia had ended up sleeping in a bath towel and brushing her teeth with her fingers at the hotel that morning. Marcia had not cared one bit—a bonus night in Miami had been just what she needed.

Marcia was now desperately trying to hang onto that "Miami feeling", or at least the Miami temps that had soaked into her skin earlier that day. She WAS feeling a bit out of place in Chicago wearing Capri's and her apple green sandals. Everyone else was wearing corduroys and chukka boots. Marcia envisioned her sandals being treated with some kind of "anti-stress" formula to protect her from the other frustrated travelers. Marcia had not yet realized that this relaxation technique was about to fail miserably.
Being stranded in the airport for the entire day, however, did have one "perk." It gave Marcia plenty of time to make the transition from the peacefulness of an ocean cruise ship to the frozen seats of her Civic Hybrid, which would undoubtedly be surrounded by noisy, grating snow plows managing the 27" of snow. Once Marcia finally arrived back in Minneapolis, she still needed to make the sixty-plus mile drive to Haystack. Marcia was not looking forward to this drive and knew that, realistically, she could be on the road for hours that evening.

Marcia decided not to think about her complicated journey ahead and made a conscious effort to find a more pleasant train of thought - GUSTAV. She was quite pleased overall with the outcome of the "Gustav message board scheme." The fact that Luscious had been able to locate Gustav's message board and that Marcia had actually had the confidence to leave her contact info was encouraging. There WAS a chance that Gustav would connect the dots and actually CALL HER. Replaying her seventh deck ship conversation with Gustav now allowed Marcia to tune out all the angry voices around her. The thought of Gustav's gentle voice helped her keep the "post-vacation blues" at bay.

Cheered by the thought of a potential phone call from Gustav, Marcia decided she had better take the plunge and check her email. Her daughter had probably sent mail, and she was SURE her FACESPACE.COM Inbox would be overflowing with replies to her "PINK.ROC.DOC" snippet. She can only imagine how her gal pals have reacted to such an outrageous idea. Marcia smiled at this thought until suddenly, it dawned on her–"PINK. ROC.DOC" was now "PUBLIC INFO!" If Rodney had responded to her FACESPACE.COM friend request while Marcia was away, he would then have had access to "PINK.ROC.DOC!" The very same "PINK.ROC. DOC" she had proudly (and spontaneously) posted to her FACESPACE. COM profile before she left town. Marcia cringed with this sudden realization. "OMG, OMG, OMG, SH--, OMG!" How could she have been so impulsive? It was typical Marcia behavior.

All dreamy thoughts of Gustav immediately flew out the grimy airport window. BREEAATTHHHE, Marcia, she told herself. BREEAATHE. It was impossible for Marcia to breathe. "OMG, OMG, OMG, SH--, OMG!" The ramifications of this lapse in judgment were staggering. Rodney, by simply "be-friending" Marcia, could potentially have figured out by now that Marcia was TOTALLY IN LOVE WITH HIM! How could Marcia not have thought this through more carefully?

In a daze, Marcia fumbled for her laptop case and extracted "Granny." There was no sense in putting off the inevitable. Marcia may as well find out if Rodney was now privy to "PINK.ROC.DOC" and, potentially, her feelings for him. Marcia tried to convince herself that Rodney would not have been able to make such a "leap" just by reading "PINK.ROC. DOC." In fact, Marcia was convinced that Rodney would not even have taken the time to READ "PINK.ROC.DOC!" After all, guys did not THINK like women. Guys generally needed ideas SPELLED OUT VERY CLEARLY. Marcia would have had to insert Rodney's name IN BOLDED CAPITAL LETTERS throughout "PINK.ROC.DOC" in order for him to catch on. Especially since Rodney had not seen her for 32 years! Rodney would have done exactly what other men would do–looked carefully at her profile photos and quickly skimmed through her vital info. Unlike Marcia, Rodney would not have spent countless hours absorbing every tidbit of info on Marcia's FACESPACE.COM profile. Once Marcia had consoled herself with these thoughts, she began to breathe a little easier.

By now, "Granny" was powered up and ready to use. Once Marcia had read the email messages from her daughter, she immediately logged onto FACESPACE.COM. Her Inbox had 22 New Messages. Marcia stared at the screen for a full five minutes without touching the keyboard. Marcia was scared to even contemplate reading her first FACESPACE.COM message. Even worse, Marcia knew she was going to have to weed through all 22 messages to determine if Rodney had replied to her friend request.

Marcia was not sure that she was up to this task. Marcia was so sure that she was NOT up to this task that she promptly powered off her laptop and slid "Granny" back into her laptop case. All Marcia was sure of, at this point in the stressful day, is that she needed a LARGE Bloody Mary from the airport bar before she could tackle her FACESPACE.COM messages. What would be worse, she thought - further FACESPACE.COM friend rejection from Rodney, or some chilling indication that Rodney had read "PINK.ROC.DOC?"

A short time later, emboldened by the emergency Bloody Mary, Marcia powered up "Granny" a second time. By now, she had worked the "Rodney Rumination" through in her mind. Really, all she had done was sent a simple request to Rodney, asking him to be her friend. At this point, she still had no clue if Rodney had even accepted her as a friend.

If, however, Rodney HAD read "PINK.ROC.DOC" (and by some twist of fate realized that Marcia was referring to him), then Marcia was in BIG trouble. Rodney would be scared sh--less! Rodney would have, by now, run for the hills! Even though "PINK.ROC.DOC" was just a fantasy, an idea thought up by a woman who happened to spend most of her time in "La La Land."

Men were, after all, notorious for requiring ample "processing time" when faced with any written or verbal text that posed a romantic "threat." This was especially true when the words threatened a man's sense of being "in charge." Marcia did not think Rodney was an exception to this phenomenon. In fact, Marcia intuited that Rodney was the kind of guy who needed standard "processing time" times six. Heck, due to the serious nature of "PINK.ROC.DOC", Rodney might need standard "processing time" times sixty! Sadly enough, this could be the real reason why Rodney had not yet replied to Marcia, not the fact that she had thrown up on his shoes thirty years earlier. Marcia might NEVER hear back from Rodney. Marcia now had to steel herself, gird her loins, accept this as a possible outcome and somehow move on.

Marcia was jolted back into reality by this thought. "Granny" was waiting on Marcia. "Granny" had limited battery time left. Marcia returned to her Inbox and began to browse through her FACESPACE.COM mail. Her eyes scanned each message header without even processing the accompanying text. All she cared about, at this point, was seeing who the reply was actually FROM. Gal Pal #1 had sent mail, Gal Pal #2, Gal Pal #3, Gal Pal #4...but NO reply from RODNEY. BREEAATTHHHE, Marcia, she told herself. Gal Pal #5 had sent mail, Gal Pal #6, Gal Pal #7... Marcia continued on until she got to the message from Gal Pal #19 and then suddenly she stopped. "OMG, OMG - NO REPLY FROM RODNEY - OMG, SH--, OMG!" There were only three emails left to check. Marcia's heart was pounding. In fact, she even had to wipe an errant tear from her eye. This was more than she could endure at the freaking Chicago airport gate. Marcia felt like this was really IT–if there was no friend response from Rodney, all was lost.

At this point, Marcia was blinking back multiple tears. She had to wiggle her toes just to keep herself from having a full-fledged meltdown in front of hundreds of strangers at the Chicago airport. She clicked on her last Inbox message. Suddenly, Marcia's heart was no longer pounding. Marcia's heart had stopped beating. There, on the dimming "Granny" laptop screen were the two words from Rodney that she had longed for–"I ACCEPT." Not only had Rodney approved Marcia's friend request, he had even taken the time to put the response into his own words–"I ACCEPT." Marcia stared at her laptop screen in disbelief. Before she could even begin to comprehend Rodney's reply, she realized that she was being paged by the airline attendant standing behind the check-in desk. Marcia promptly powered off "Granny" and, in a daze, walked toward the airline desk.

Now Marcia was back in "La La Land" at 30,000 feet in the air. Her wild imagination had taken off with Flight 444. She was currently occupying herself by reviewing EVERY possible reason why she was so smitten with Rodney. Why she felt so SURE about Rodney. Even though she had not seen him for thirty-two years, nor did she have a freaking clue what was going on in his life. None of this mattered to Marcia. In fact, by now Marcia had fully convinced herself that Rodney was her BOY-FOR-ALL-SEASONS (B-F-A-S)!

MARCIA CONVENIENTLY IGNORED ANY "RED FLAGS" SHE HAD GOTTEN FROM RODNEY'S FACESPACE.COM PROFILE (THEREBY AVOIDING REALITY). ONLY MARCIA, THE ONE-EARRING POSTER GIRL FOR THE "PIRATES OF PASSION" LONELY HEARTS CLUB COULD CONVINCE HERSELF OF UNREQUITED LOVE WITH A MAN SHE HAD NOT SEEN FOR 32 FREAKING YEARS!

MARCIA'S PERTINENT "NON-FACTS" REGARDING RODNEY:

1. RODNEY WAS EXTREMELY CONSIDERATE
    Marcia was SO touched by the fact that Rodney had taken the time to compose his own message to her. Even if it was only two words. Those two beautifully constructed words–"I ACCEPT"–meant the WORLD to Marcia. They were a confirmation of everything Marcia remembered about the "REAL" Rodney. Marcia had, by this time, worked herself into a complete LATHER over Rodney. She was totally able to disregard the fact that she had been waiting on Rodney for weeks. Marcia was in an uncharacteristic state of forgiveness only because Marcia's head was in the CLOUDS.

2. RODNEY WAS A "ROCK."
    Rodney was strong and secure and, most of all, Rodney was CALM. Marcia, on any given day, went from laughing hysterically over cowboy names to crying tears of despair while doing her downward dog yoga pose. Rodney would be the perfect complement to Marcia's high-strung, driven, psycho-woman nature. Even with Marcia's personality flaws, Rodney would appreciate the way Marcia could light up a room when he was with her. Rodney would realize that Marcia was one-of-a-kind and love her for who she really was! Rodney would be the one man who would be able to CALM MARCIA DOWN! Rodney would always be there for Marcia.

3. RODNEY WAS WELL-TRAVELED
    Based on his forty-four gorgeous FACESPACE.COM travel scrapbooks, Rodney had been all over the world. Marcia, too, had traveled extensively, LOVED to travel. Marcia had a pretty impressive travel scrapbook herself and had even lived abroad.

Rodney would impress Marcia with his travel stories and invite her to join him on trips to Singapore and Stockholm and Stavanger and Sydney. Every time Marcia glanced down at the mini-travel-suitcase of mints that she had gotten on Flight 444, she could not help but fantasize about traveling with Rodney, staying in upscale hotels around the world and spending time in first-class airplane seats together, sipping champagne.

4. RODNEY WAS ADORABLE
    In fact, Rodney was near-perfect, in looks and stature. Rodney had something about him that was irresistible to Marcia. It was hard to put into words. Every time Marcia saw her favorite photo of Rodney, she yearned to be near him. Part of Rodney's appeal, Marcia thought, was that he downplayed his near-perfectness so well. (In the back of Marcia's mind loomed the realization that Marcia was in total denial because Rodney had become a FREAKING PLAYER!)

    Marcia immediately justified this realization with her gut feeling that Rodney was not really, in his heart, a FREAKING PLAYER. Rodney had simply been thrown off-course by the 156 female friends on his FACESPACE.COM profile. Rodney had been led astray for years by these beautiful women, only to discover that they were somewhat shallow. These women did not really care about Rodney's inner strength and beauty. Marcia would be the woman who could help Rodney to DISCOVER WHO HE REALLY WAS! Marcia had, by now, totally talked herself out of the entire "RODNEY-AS-PLAYER" concept. Marcia was completely ready to convince Rodney that he was her BOY-FOR-ALL-SEASONS.

Marcia felt confident that the "PINK.ROC.DOC" dilemma would work itself out. Marcia had options. She could always "play dumb" with Rodney and act as though "PINK.ROC.DOC" had absolutely nothing to do with him. Marcia had to rely on her natural charm and wit to convince Rodney that "PINK.ROC.DOC" had not been written with him in mind. Although Marcia was pretty sure Rodney would remember what a wild imagination she had. Heck, Rodney might even feel FLATTERED by the thought of such a hare-brained idea written with him in mind! Marcia

Elaine Hoover

was going to do her best to remain calm and try not to think about the ramifications of her "PINK.ROC.DOC" slip-up. She decided now that she had better compose herself and try to get some rest before landing in "blizzard hell."

MARCH 21–SUNDAY (CONTINUED)
DAYS SINCE MUSIC CRUISE=1
DAYS SINCE PROMISE OF CALL FROM IRISH=N/A
MARCIA COULD LIVE WITHOUT RACING COVERALLS.
REPLACED WITH POTENTIAL CALL FROM GUSTAV IN
GERMANY!
DAYS SINCE FRIEND REQUEST CONFIRMED BY RODNEY=0
**MARCIA'S BEVVIE-OF-THE-MOMENT=PATRON SILVER
TEQUILA MARGARITAS SERVED IN AN ASSORTMENT OF
GLASSWARE**
BRANDI'S LYRICS (VIA HEADPHONES) THAT GET HER
THRU=I'M HAPPY CAN'T YOU SEE, I'M ALRIGHT

Marcia was exhausted and, at the same time, elated. Her post-flight journey home had been every bit as treacherous as she had imagined it would be. By the time she reached Haystack, she was a nervous wreck. In her usual caffeine-addict fashion, Marcia had picked up a "to-go" coffee in Minneapolis, thinking it would help her navigate the blizzard-ish road conditions. But since she was unfamiliar with the design of the cup's lid, most of the coffee had ended up in her lap. Marcia spent the next sixty miles in a sodden state. She was so happy to pull into her driveway after the long travel day. A hot shower and her favorite polka dot pajamas would feel so good.

For a change, her driveway was actually plowed. As Marcia eased cautiously into the garage, she noticed something sitting on her front porch. Because it was covered in snow, it was impossible to make out what is was. Marcia made a mental note to check the front porch once she had gotten the furnace cranked up and had changed into her PJ's.

Once she had gotten into lounge mode, refreshed and pink-cheeked from a scalding shower, Marcia decided it was time for a celebratory margarita. She had several reasons to celebrate. The fact that she had made it home to her cozy condo versus spending the night in the airport was reason enough. The fact that there had been good news from Rodney in her "Inbox" after such a long, tormented wait was also worth celebrating. To Marcia, Rodney's simple words–"I ACCEPT"– represented hope. Hope that there really were still some NICE guys left in the world. Marcia had never given up on the "nice guy" concept. She wasn't sure why she continued to believe in this ideal, especially after recently reviewing her painful "track record." Yet she had come to the conclusion that this was something she really LIKED about herself–Marcia was not going to become a cynical old maid like other women she knew. Ultimately, it did not matter what the outcome of her "hidden agenda" (aka "PINK.ROCK.DOC") with Rodney turned out to be. Rodney, to her, represented possibility–and for Marcia, that was enough.

Suddenly, Marcia remembered she had forgotten to check what was sitting on the front porch. The "mystery" package. It took a few minutes for her to dig through the snow and determine what was frozen to her cement stoop. "OMG, OMG, OMG, SH--, OMG!" There, encrusted with ice, lay a bouquet of gorgeous pink roses! PINK roses–her favorite! Marcia had a fleeting thought–could Gustav have sent the lovely roses? That made absolutely no sense–Gustav knew that she was just returning from the cruise. Marcia carefully scooped the roses out from the snow drift. Miraculously, they seemed alive, unaffected by the sub-zero temps. Who the hell would be sending me roses, Marcia wondered. As if in answer, a small white envelope fell from the flowers. Marcia picked it up and peered at it in the semi-darkness. All she could see was her name printed neatly on the outside of the envelope. Marcia's heart began to race. She put the envelope in her pajama pocket and double-checked the ice and snow to make sure she hadn't missed anything. "OMG, OMG, OMG, SH--, OMG!" There, hidden deeper under the snow, was a brown Fed X package. Marcia stared at the package for a moment in disbelief. Then she decisively scooped up the package and the roses and returned to the warmth of her living room. She carefully placed the semi-frozen flowers into her favorite vase to thaw. Marcia realized she was definitely going to need ALCOHOL before she had the nerve to open either the package OR the envelope in her pajama pocket.

Marcia peered into her cupboard and was rewarded by the reassuring sight of her Patron Silver tequila. The very same Imported 100% AGAVE tequila that had set her back an astonishing $42.99. Top-of-the-line tequila that Marcia had rewarded herself with before the cruise for finishing a major section of her novel aka blockbuster screenplay. Marcia had NEVER before bought herself such an extravagant bottle of tequila. It had been the most expensive bottle of tequila in the Haystack municipal liquor store. Marcia was now extremely grateful that she had splurged on the best tequila and that she still had some left in her cupboard. The way the night was shaping up, Marcia was going to need more than ONE celebratory margarita.

Marcia immediately got busy, intent on blending the perfect margarita. It was important to create a festive atmosphere when working with such an extravagant bottle of alcohol. The scene of her congratulatory margarita soon became such a sight to behold that Marcia could not resist taking a picture of it. The countertop held her special green "Gorditos" shot glass from Puerto Vallarta, Mexico. The lime green detail on the shot class tied in perfectly with the lime accents on the bottle of $42.99 Patron. The lime green tissue paper from inside the Patron box made the whole margarita "set-up scene" even livelier. In the background, her miniature "bunny" tea set (black with orange carrot detail) and her treasured family memento—a Joseph Hoover beer mug—added to the festive look. Marcia was now ready to pour her celebratory margarita into her special crystal wine aka margarita glass. However, given that the rubber seal in Marcia's blender was circa 1969, the freaking contents of the blender immediately oozed out of the bottom and had to be rescued. Marcia performed a rescue operation by dumping the frozen margarita into her wine glass, her shot glass, her beer mug, even her bunny tea pot. She would do anything to save the freaking Patron from running off the countertop. Marcia momentarily questioned whether the "Patron purchase" had been such a good idea after all, given the state of her blender. She quickly dismissed this thought and, without hesitation, downed all of the available forms of margarita on her counter.

Once Marcia had ingested her top-of-the-line margaritas, she felt much calmer. Her thoughts turned to the envelope from the now-thawed bouquet of roses, as well as the Fed X package. She decided to tackle the package first. Marcia could not think of a better way to end her vacation than spending the evening opening mystery prizes. She ripped open the box and smiled when she saw the contents. A three-pound box of See's dark chocolate caramels! Her very absolute favorite See's confection! (Well, she was also partial to See's California Brittle but, no matter, the key was SEE'S dark chocolate!). "OMG," Marcia thought, "this is unbelievable." Who could possibly know that she loved See's candy? It had to be her baby sister - only her sister was privy to Marcia's "See's fetish." In fact, her sister SHARED Marcia's fetish. Marcia was stumped. Had someone seen her drive one hundred and twenty miles round-trip to the See's candy kiosk in the cities just for a "fix?" Why would her sister send her See's chocolates out of the blue? The answer resided in Marcia's pocket. Marcia must work up the courage to open the freaking card. She would not sleep until she had resolved the mystery.

A few hours later, Marcia sat on the living room floor, surrounded by empty See's caramel wrappers and the bottle of Patron. She had skipped the blender process altogether in order to minimize waste of her precious Patron. Unfortunately, she had already consumed one-quarter of the bottle of Patron just to prepare herself for the big moment of truth. She reached into her pajama pocket now for the mystery envelope. Marcia was as ready as she would ever be. She carefully opened the envelope and slid out the tiny card. What she saw written on the card made her gasp! In bold, block letters was one word–R O D N E Y. Marcia was in shock! This was more than she could comprehend. Not only had Rodney "befriended" her, he had taken it to a whole new level and sent her treats. Not just any treats– See's dark chocolates! Marcia's favorite kind of treats! How did Rodney know what her favorite treats were? And what, exactly, was Rodney's intent by sending her such extravagant treats? Was he simply feeling guilty for not befriending her in a timely manner? Or was Rodney trying to show that he, too, was smitten? It was just like Rodney not to write anything in the card except for his name. This meant Marcia would now spend hours pondering the meaning behind the roses and chocolates. Marcia decided that she was going to need a clear head to try and figure out the significance of Rodney's gifts. She had better cork the bottle of Patron and attempt to get some sleep.

MARCH 22–MONDAY
DAYS SINCE MUSIC CRUISE=2
DAYS SINCE PROMISE OF CALL FROM IRISH=N/A
DAYS SINCE POTENTIAL CALL FROM GUSTAV IN GERMANY=N/A
DAYS SINCE FRIEND REQUEST CONFIRMED BY RODNEY=1
MARCIA'S BEVVIE-OF-THE-MOMENT=STRONG FRENCH ROAST WITH 1/2 & 1/2
BRANDI'S LYRICS (VIA HEADPHONES) THAT GET HER THRU=I'M HAPPY CAN'T YOU SEE, I'M ALRIGHT

The next morning, Marcia awoke early. Even with a gigantic Patron hangover, she was able to tackle the "Rodney dilemma." Marcia's first instinct had been to write Rodney a lengthy FACESPACE.COM message. But Marcia reconsidered and decided, for once in her life, to write absolutely NOTHING to Rodney. Rodney was probably just overridden with guilt. She would not share with him how touched she was by the prizes left on her doorstep. She would not tell him ANY of the million sweet, mushy thoughts she was having about him. She would not tell him that she had dreamt about him all night. She certainly would not tell him that he had been on her mind from the moment she woke up that morning. Marcia would employ an entirely different "strategy" with Rodney and not tell him ANYTHING. She would just keep her mouth shut. Marcia was not going to jump to any conclusions. It was obvious that Rodney knew how to contact her. It would be totally up to Rodney to make the next move.

MARCH 26–FRIDAY

DAYS SINCE MUSIC CRUISE=6

DAYS SINCE PROMISE OF CALL FROM IRISH=N/A

DAYS SINCE POTENTIAL CALL FROM GUSTAV IN GERMANY=N/A

DAYS SINCE FRIEND REQUEST CONFIRMED BY RODNEY=5

MARCIA'S BEVVIE-OF-THE-MOMENT=STRONG FRENCH ROAST WITH 1/2 & 1/2

BRANDI'S LYRICS (VIA HEADPHONES) THAT GET HER THRU=I'M HAPPY CAN'T YOU SEE, I'M ALRIGHT

Over the next several days, Marcia continued to stand by her decision not to contact Rodney. There were times when Betty had to physically restrain Marcia from clicking on the FACESPACE.COM "Send" button. Marcia always seemed to have thoughts to share with Rodney. When this occurred, she simply recorded her thoughts in a FACESPACE.COM message and saved it in her "Draft" folder instead. It was unlike Marcia to feel so timid. It was unlike Marcia not to impulsively send mail to Rodney.

Betty, after hearing Marcia's incredible front step story, was astonished by Marcia's resolve not to contact Rodney. Both women, however, knew enough about how men behaved that they should NEVER try and figure out the meaning behind a man's actions. Marcia would be better off if she did not try to make up any sort of explanation for Rodney's behavior. Chances were that Marcia would be so far off the mark, it would be laughable. Betty consoled Marcia with the fact that, should she EVER hear from Rodney again, Marcia would then be able to deluge Rodney with all of her drafted "love letters." Rodney would then have time to appreciate all of her heartfelt thoughts. For now, Marcia was not even sure Rodney deserved any validation of her feelings. The "PINK.ROCK.DOC" dilemma would live on—with one difference. It was no longer Marcia's dilemma.

Granted, Marcia went through not one, but several bottles of Patron during this period. Rodney, however, did not need to know that. Marcia had learned to "play it cool" and was actually having quite a bit of fun with it. Any time she was tempted to send Rodney Draft #1 (#2, #3, #4, #5…) she would simply read through the message and realize how much Rodney was missing. She imagined being the recipient of such thoughtful, flattering, kind words and by some form of reverse logic, this made her feel better. Once Marcia had gotten her daily "love letter" to Rodney out of her system, she was able to throw herself into her work (record whisk sales, record progress on her blockbuster novel aka screenplay) and simply forget about Rodney.

Later that night, Marcia returned from a GNO (Girls Night Out) only to spot another "mystery package" on her doorstep. Her heart began to thump loudly. Do NOT get yourself all worked up, Marcia told herself. It could be anything. It could be new phone books. Or her 10-box order of Girl Scout Thin Mints. The package did not resemble a box of See's chocolates in the least (secretly, Marcia was disappointed—she had scarfed her 3 pounds of dark chocolate caramels in record time and had been craving them ever since). This package was in a larger, non-descript box and had arrived through the standard mail, not via Fed X. Marcia's name had been carefully printed in block letters. There was no return address. Marcia picked up the package, expecting it to be heavy, but it was not. The weightlessness of the box only added to the intrigue. Marcia could not wait to get it inside and open it.

Once she had settled herself in her quiet living room with a glass of red wine, Marcia tore into the package. She peeked inside—the box appeared to be filled with nothing other than lime green tissue paper! Marcia was confused. Why would someone go through all the trouble of sending her a box full of tissue paper? She ran her hands along the bottom of the box to make sure she hadn't missed something. In the far corner of the box, she felt a small, flat item. It was a generic CD case. Stuck to the case was a yellow Post-It note with the instructions, "Play this first." Marcia gingerly lifted the CD from its case and stared at it for a long moment. She looked back down at the CD case. There, in the otherwise-empty liner, sat a folded piece of copy paper with the words, "Read while listening to Track #1." There was no signature on the paper—only a carefully drawn smiley face. Marcia felt a bit unsettled. Who would be sending her a CD? Could it possibly be from—OMG— Rodney?

She decided she had nothing to lose by inserting the CD into her player and cranking up the volume. The opening notes of the first song sounded very familiar to her. Marcia smiled and unfolded the accompanying sheet of paper. It took her a few minutes to figure out what she was looking at.

Just then, the refrain of the song–"Stay the Night"–broke through her thoughts. Suddenly everything clicked. The paper Marcia held in her hand was a freaking MAP. Not only a map, but a map to Rodney's up-north Wisconsin hideaway!

Marcia dropped the map in disbelief. Wow. NEVER in her life had she imagined anything like THIS arriving on her doorstep. Marcia had followed her gut feeling and pushed Rodney to the back of her mind. She felt no regret. It had gotten to the point where the memory of "PINK.ROCK. DOC" only made her laugh. She laughed because she was pretty sure she had made Rodney laugh. She laughed because it was safe to assume that Rodney had never "received" such a creative, unique, outrageous message from a female before. She laughed because she knew, in her heart, that Rodney would NEVER forget such a crazy message. Rodney would never forget her.

Marcia felt no urgent need to run and start packing her bags. She did not feel the need to pick up the phone and call Betty either. Marcia felt, instead, a sense of peacefulness. She could wait to study the map Rodney had sent to her. For now, Marcia wanted to savor the magic of the music. Rodney had started off his extraordinary CD with a special song that Marcia would always associate with him. But the special songs did not end there. Rodney had actually taken the time to create an ENTIRE CD OF SONGS JUST FOR HER! To Marcia, there was no greater honor. In Marcia's eyes, the essence of a hopeless romantic was the ability to express their feelings through music. Any man that would do that for Marcia obviously "got her", got what made her tick. For tonight, at least, this was enough for Marcia. She would go to bed listening to song lyrics dedicated just to HER and dream of the moment she and Rodney would share a romantic night together, whisking each other's delectable scalps.

FIVE MONTHS LATER...

AUGUST 26–THURSDAY
DAYS SINCE MUSIC CRUISE=133
DAYS SINCE MARCIA BECAME LOVESTRUCK=133
MARCIA'S BEVVIE-OF-THE-MOMENT=STRONG FRENCH ROAST WITH 1/2 & 1/2
BRANDI'S LYRICS (VIA HEADPHONES) THAT GET HER THRU=I'M HAPPY CAN'T YOU SEE, I'M ALRIGHT

OH, SH--! Marcia stood up and flung the Cartier catalog that she gripped tightly in her hand directly out her back door. The catalog hit the "FOR SALE–BANK OWNED" sign that was propped on the empty lot adjacent to Marcia's quaint "DOLL HOUSE" condo.

Marcia took a deep breath. Her short-term memory was definitely going south. The pink diamond engagement ring that Rodney the "Rock" had purchased for their October dream wedding and open air rock concert in Red Rock Canyon was, in reality, a FREAKING PINK DIAMOND BRACELET! And NOT 15.21 carats as Marcia had remembered - it was 36 carats plus (oop-dee, that was asking a bit much, even from sweet, steady Rodney the "Rock"). But shipping WAS included!

BUT WAIT! Marcia could always have it sized...or... she could have it made into a ring AND a bracelet! Just thinking of the overabundance of pink, sparkly jewels adorning her finger and wrist made her smile (she deliberately ignored the voice in her head that told her the sacred covenant of marriage was NOT about the size and color of the ring and matching bonus bracelet). But ... Marcia DID had small fingers. She COULD pull this off! Marcia sighed contentedly and headed out the back door to retrieve the dog-eared catalog.

To Uncle Pete, whose Xmas money funded the laptop, the zip drive and the dark chocolate.

To all other German and Norwegian spirits who hover nearby.

To the original bad date book - may it R.I.P.

To daughter "Ann", the amazing artist, writer, fashion designer, musician and aspiring psychologist – my biggest inspiration of all.

To Brandi Carlile, for her blue-moon inspiration.

To "soul-sis-tah" Susan and Dino and Madge for their ongoing support and help making the author believe in herself.

To Jul, for always being there and to Roy, for providing the headphones.

To "Betty" for providing one-liner material.

To the original "Cayamo Cal-gals"–Jennifer, Jill and Nicole.

To "Right-Click Rodney", for the inspiration provided from "the photo."

To Ari Hest, for use of "The Weight" lyrics.

To Stephanie and Sara and the gang at Willowbridge, for the scalp "whisk".

To SeBrina, Shawn and Cully for providing "the escapes".

To the "twinkies" Andrea and Kaylie, my pseudo-daughters.